Love is
a time of enchantment:
in it all days are fair and all fields
green. Youth is blest by it,
old age made benign: the eyes of love see
roses blooming in December,
and sunshine through rain. Verily
is the time of true-love
a time of enchantment—and
Oh! how eager is woman
to be bewitched!

MOONLIGHT AND MARCH ROSES

Lynn's search to trace a missing girl takes her to Spain where she meets Clive Hendon—also on the case. They come to an uneasy working arrangement and begin to know one another as individuals. While untangling the situation round the girl's disappearance, Lynn untangles her emotions and decides on her own future.

Books by D. Y. Cameron
in the Ulverscroft Large Print Series:

A PUZZLED HEART
ENCHANTING ADVENTURE
CONFLICTING TIDES
THE HAPPY AWAKENING
MOONLIGHT AND MARCH ROSES

D. Y. CAMERON

MOONLIGHT AND MARCH ROSES

Complete and Unabridged

ULVERSCROFT
Leicester

First published in Great Britain in 1970 by
Robert Hale Ltd.,
London

First Large Print Edition
published September 1990

British Library CIP Data

Cameron, D. Y.
    Moonlight and March roses.—Large print ed.—
Ulverscroft large print series: romance, suspense
I. Title
823'.914[F]

ISBN 0-7089-2280-5

Published by
F. A. Thorpe (Publishing) Ltd.
Anstey, Leicestershire
Set by Rowland Phototypesetting Ltd.
Bury St. Edmunds, Suffolk
Printed and bound in Great Britain by
T. J. Press (Padstow) Ltd., Padstow, Cornwall

1

" **A**LL right. I will." Lynn looked at the elegant, middle-aged woman sitting opposite her on the other side of the desk and heard the words repeat in her mind as she said them. She was aware of a slight sense of shock.

She was receptionist/secretary to Hendon's Personal Service Bureau, and at Mrs. Tracey's request had given her this interview.

Lynn licked her lips. It wasn't her job to interview clients. It was not her job to commit herself as she had done by agreeing to help Mrs. Tracey.

"All right, I will," she said again with a trace of defiance in her voice. For the moment she didn't realise the full implication of the words but she did sense that they would change the pattern of her life.

She smiled, a warm friendly smile and appreciated the relief that flooded Mrs. Tracey's face. She was a reserved woman conscious of the appearance she showed to

1

the world so that the relief was more revealing than it might have been. Automatically Lynn registered the impression. She hadn't worked for Hendon's for five years without learning to use her eyes and make her own judgements. Both had become second nature in her business life.

"I don't know how to say thank you . . ." Mrs. Tracey shook her head.

Lynn also shook hers—at herself. She didn't know what had come over her to make her behave so impetuously, but now wasn't the time to examine her motives. She had committed herself. "The thanks will come later," she said briskly, to lower the emotional temperature, and added almost in a panic and half hoping for an escape route, "you're quite *sure* you want me to take over the case personally?"

"Quite sure." Mrs. Tracey's voice was firm.

"All right then." To her own ears her voice sounded weak but Mrs. Tracey didn't seem to notice. She looked at Lynn expectantly.

Lynn looked at her and then pulled forward a pad. She had the file on her desk but felt she needed a pen in her hand and a pad before her to give a focal point as she asked questions.

Mrs. Tracey had first come to Hendon's Personal Service Bureau a month ago. Her daughter, an only child, was missing and she had enlisted Hendon's help to find her.

Lynn doodled on the pad. On the surface it had appeared to be a straightforward case of a missing person, one that would be solved in time without too many complications. Joan Tracey was twenty-two. Presumably she had grown tired of a somewhat sheltered home life—where she'd been spoilt—and gone off on her own. Such cases often solved themselves by the missing person walking in at the front door one day . . .

Lynn went on doodling.

"Joan was so happy. She had everything she could want at home. Everything."

Lynn's hazel eyes looked into Mrs. Tracey's face and wondered. It wasn't likely Joan would have acted as she did if she had been happy. One had to be quite unhappy to act so deliberately.

"I've got the story here, of course. All the facts are in the file. But . . . I'd like to go over them myself with you."

"I can't tell you any more. I just can't think what made her do it." Mrs. Tracey was genuinely puzzled. "She could have had anything. Her father was going to buy her a new car."

"She didn't take her car with her?"

"No. When she first left, she said she was so near her work that she could walk to the hospital."

Lynn knew it all, of course. She had taken the reports from both Ellis and Clive Hendon who'd worked on the case, and typed them back. Joan Tracey, after a discussion with her parents—it couldn't even be called an argument according to Mrs. Tracey—had left home to live in a bedsitter and had taken a job in the records department of the local General Hospital.

After a few months she had moved to the North of England where she'd taken a similar job.

"She wrote twice a week at first." Mrs. Tracey's voice was uncomprehending as she continued, "Then only once and then the letters became fewer and fewer, and now . . ."

"Yes. Yes," Lynn nodded hurriedly.

4

Joan Tracey had left her digs in North Faldon and she had not left a forwarding address. The Traceys had visited her landlady who could tell them nothing and no efforts so far had been successful in picking up a trace of the girl. Mrs. Tracey had come to Hendon's a month ago. Now they were washing their hands of the case —nicely, of course, saying that it wasn't ethical to continue taking the Traceys' money with no, or very little hope, of success. That was one of the factors that puzzled Lynn. It wasn't like either of the Hendon brothers to give up while there was one stone unturned. Clive, the younger, was particularly tenacious, yet in this case his was the voice that had been most insistent that the file should be marked closed and put among the very few unsolved cases.

When Mrs. Tracey had gone, Lynn sat at the desk thinking, thinking about the Tracey home life, thinking logically and unemotionally but not unsympathetically —especially towards Joan. She was aware in a slight way of a fellow feeling. Life at home could be difficult . . .

She pushed the dark, near black, hair

off her forehead and stared unseeing at the doodles on her pad.

Hendon's Personal Service Bureau was a successful detective agency run by two brothers. Evelyn Laurel—Lynn—had been with them for five years, since she had come with first class references to take the post of Receptionist/Secretary. Now? That was still her official title though she was far more part of the firm than her post suggested. She had a quick brain and a natural aptitude for sorting relevant data. She was often able to give Clive or Ellis a new slant on a case that had got bogged down.

That hadn't happened in the Tracey case. Ellis had begun on it, then passed it over to Clive who, suddenly it seemed, had decided there was nothing more Hendon's could do.

And now she had agreed to take on the case privately.

"You must be mad," she told herself and felt a sinking in the pit of her stomach as she began to see what it would mean.

She'd have to leave Hendon's.

The door from the vestibule burst open and Lynn looked up knowing who she

6

would see. No one else ever entered in the same breezy way as Clive Hendon.

"Hallo, no tea?"

Lynn frowned at the clock. It was quarter to four.

"You're slipping."

If he did but know! Lynn thought to herself with an upsurge of excitement. She felt Clive glance at her but she hadn't time to raise her eyebrows and return look for look. There was the afternoon cuppa to be made. Weak for Ellis, strong for Clive, medium for her.

"Get the cups," she commanded.

"Petticoat government," he grunted and strolled to the cupboard. Clive never walked if he could stroll. He never did anything in a conventional way if he could do it colourfully. Lynn paused with the warmed teapot as she waited for the kettle to boil. The adjective she would apply to Clive was confident. He wasn't assertive, aggressive or cocky, but he was self-confident. He saw the world as his oyster.

Lynn made the tea and filled a flask with some to water down Ellis's cup. He'd be in shortly.

A smile curved her well-defined lips.

7

For a year before coming to the bureau she had worked in a big office where the work was streamlined and the tea, provided by an outside firm of caterers, came round on a trolley—and no working minutes were lost. Here . . . The smile widened. She was paid an awful lot to include tea-making as one of her jobs.

"Now what?" Clive asked interestedly.

"I was thinking."

"Whose case?" Clive was always ready to listen if she'd had a hunch.

"No one's. Tea," she explained and brought the ready laughter to his lips. Clive enjoyed life and brought a zest to work and play. He didn't believe it was necessary to be serious to do serious work, and his results proved his theory. It was very seldom that one of his cases had to be marked closed without being brought to a satisfactory conclusion—not happy necessarily Lynn admitted. They were dealing with life in the Hendon Bureau, with men and women not cardboard figures.

"What about the tea?" he asked sugaring his liberally. He had keen eyes for all his laughing, easy manner and they

8

looked at her curiously. Lynn had never been able to decide if they were grey-blue or blue-grey. "Now what?" he asked with exaggerated patience.

"You'd be surprised," she answered and thought how true was that usually meaningless phrase.

"I don't know," he retorted with masculine self-assurance. "You're not a surprising person. You come up with the odd idea now and again that's right out of the blue and hits the nail on the head, but I shouldn't have said, basically, you were a person of surprises. Where's Ellis?"

"He said he'd be in about four." He was the senior and boss of Hendon's, and Lynn started typing, dismissing Clive as lightly as he had done her. So she wasn't surprising? Well, she didn't know that it was a particularly desirable thing to be when you thought about it rationally. Not to be able to rely on a person . . . Cut it, Lynn ordered herself. What had got under her skin was the way Clive had said it. He made her sound dull.

"I'll wait for him in the office. Can you give me the Maxwell file."

Lynn found it, gave Ellis his tea when

he came in and let her mind examine her own position.

She had accepted a temporary job that was going to take all she had to bring it to a satisfactory conclusion; it would also mean leaving the Bureau, a good permanent job that she liked. It would be unethical to stay, even if the Hendons would let her.

A pretty poor exchange, Lynn admitted, but she didn't feel as dismayed as she ought. For over a year now she had been saying to herself, "One day . . ."

On that "one day" she was going to step out, to make a new life, she always thought dreamily. She wasn't a dreamer all the time. She was practical and it was that streak in her that had for so long prevented her from realising her dream of freedom. Now? She believed she had burnt her boats.

She was half-smiling as she reviewed the situation and sorted the facts to docket them systematically in her mind.

She was twenty-four. She didn't take a mirror from her handbag to check the next facts, she had seen her face often enough to be able to assess her looks. They'd never sink a battleship but she had an attractive face as she had been told many times, and fellows seemed to like it. She had very dark shiny smooth hair, bright hazel eyes that flashed from gold to green when she was excited and had a slightly oriental slant. She was vivacious when she was happy and uninhibited—and she could talk a lot! She was also a good secretary who knew when to keep her mouth shut.

She should be able to get another job easily. Her home at Gordon Green was only five miles from the City and within easy reach of any job she might get in London.

Gordon Green was a pleasant suburb. She had lived at Flat Number 5 in Hamilton Court with her mother ever since her parents had been divorced eleven years ago. Life was easy and pleasant. Father made mother a good allowance.

Those were the facts. Lynn tilted her head and looked out of the glass-topped door that opened into the vestibule.

Then she looked down at the Tracey file on her desk and read the facts again. Joan Tracey, aged twenty-two, had left a happy home and disappeared for no apparent reason. It had been a premeditated disappearance. She had severed her ties gradually by taking a job away from home, then by moving to the North of England, then by writing less and less until some months ago the letters had ceased.

And she had covered her tracks so that no one had been able to uncover them.

The first thing that struck Lynn was the fact that Joan had not been happy at home. The fact that her parents were rich and prepared to give her anything—*anything* Mrs. Tracy had said—wasn't of any consideration to Joan.

And neither were her parents' feelings. The urge to go must have been very strong.

For four years, ever since she was twenty, Lynn had dreamed of leaving home and living her own life, but the urge had never been strong enough to make her strong enough to face the emotional storm it would cause.

Her mother needed her, she said, "You're all I've got." She talked of Lynn's marriage. "Until you meet the right man this is a happy life for you, and I'll be honest, I love having you."

That was the rub. Mother loved having her. And mother was a thoroughly selfish woman. Lynn's real affection for her mother didn't blind her to that fact now though it had until a year or so ago. She had believed it was for her good that her mother never wholly approved of any of her boy friends.

"He's very nice, dear, but not what I've always dreamed of for you . . . not special enough." Mother's smile was warm. "You're a rather special person, you see."

Almost cynically Lynn nodded as she sat at her desk. Mother didn't want her to get married. She wanted her at home to be fussed over—and possessed. That was the real reason why Dad had gone. He couldn't stand being possessed.

As an only child, Lynn had accepted it without query and enjoyed being spoilt. It gave her a certain status at school to be able to say with certainty that she could have that doll, go on that outing, entertain the form at her home.

Now she saw her position clearly. She was tied to her mother's emotional apron-strings. The happy home, the friendly relationship of mother and daughter was bought at the cost of her loss of personal freedom. If she didn't break away she had come to realise with startling clarity these last weeks, she might as well resign herself to staying for ever. Too long she had been saying "Tomorrow will do . . ."

It was after her mother had gently but quite definitely in her charming way disposed of Lynn's last boy-friend that Lynn had taken stock of herself . . . and seen the warning light.

Her father always said she was too easy-going, too hopeful of affairs righting themselves, too sure that things would be different tomorrow. "They won't unless you make them, lass," he had told her last time she had visited him. "No one has the right to put his will on another person, but your mother doesn't know that."

Lynn was thinking and remembering, hearing her mother's voice, saying what she had said so many times, "I want the best for you, darling. I don't want you to make the mistake I made."

Lynn wanted the best for herself, who

didn't? But she knew she couldn't be directed to it and at last she was certain that she wasn't going to be emotionally blackmailed any longer.

Lynn dismissed her thoughts of herself and read the Tracey file but she didn't learn anything new. She made some notes and got on with her work for Clive and Ellis. Fortunately she had been up to date before Mrs. Tracey's visit as they were in a slack spell. That fact added to her surprise that Clive had declared the Tracey file closed . . . Lynn was conscious that there was something in this decision that she wanted to understand, but she knew he'd never tell her—not the truth. He'd fob her off with some flippant answer.

She shivered and switched on the extra bar of the electric fire. It had been a grey day of typically cold February weather, the sort they must expect for several weeks. It must be nice to be able to get away to the sun of the Mediterranean. As Lynn felt the warmth of the electric fire she let herself imagine it was the warmth of the sun . . .

The door from the inner office burst open. Clive, Lynn thought automatically. Ellis never came in like that.

15

"This is better. It's like the Polar regions in there. The temperature must be dropping at the rate of knots."

He ran a hand over his fair hair and shivered exaggeratedly. He was tall and willowy with a liking for bright clothes. Lynn approved of his orange shirt and green tie. She liked bright clothes herself and being dark with a clear soft complexion she could wear them. Mother hadn't approved of her red winter coat. Clive had. Lynn laughed to herself. It was the first thing she ever remembered his commenting on favourably. He had actually said he liked it—after some exaggerated wolf whistling and raised eyebrows.

Presently Ellis joined them and gave her the signed post. As she sorted it into the envelopes both brothers watched her.

"That's the lot," she said obviously as she pushed aside the last and took a deep breath. Now for it. "I should like to give in my notice."

She could feel the silence that greeted her words.

"Tomorrow is Friday. I'd like to give a week's notice and leave on Friday week." She was aware she was talking too fast but she was burning her boats and that's not an everyday action.

"Cripes," she heard Clive's breathed comment.

Ellis was slower. He looked at her as if he didn't believe he could have heard correctly. Then, "What did you say?" he asked.

She told him.

He shook his head. "Any particular reason? I mean, there's nothing wrong is there?"

"No . . . I want a change."

"Why don't you get married?" Clive asked and added sharply, "Are you? Is that why you want to leave? You've always been one for minding your own business . . ."

"Shut up, Clive." In his surprise Ellis's voice was sharp. "Nothing wrong, is there, Lynn?" He was a kindly man.

"No. Nothing. It's . . . well, it's personal. Things have come to a head, in my own mind, if you see what I mean."

"No, we don't," Clive replied. "You're muddle-headed. I don't think you know what you're doing."

Ellis was looking at her. "I think you

do, Lynn. I'm sorry you're going. There'll always be a job here for you if we can fit you in, at any time. And I'll give you references for your next job, of course." He smiled at her "I think you're wise to make a change. A change is always good for us."

Always? Lynn hoped so.

2

LYNN walked to the bus stop from the office on that Thursday thinking over the step she had taken. She would not tell her mother until tomorrow when her boats were burnt and there could be no drawing back. She nodded and used one of her commonest phrases to herself though she wasn't aware how it always coloured her reactions to life. "Tomorrow will do," she said to herself and walked along thinking of the Tracey case. There was an element of mystery that intrigued her.

If she could solve it . . . She was going to. If she didn't she'd have given up her job for nothing. No, not really. She had always known she'd have to leave Hendon's sometime. It was a pleasant and demanding job, but there was no social life to it. Gradually she had been losing touch with her school friends and she hadn't made any in her job to take their place. Of course she and Mother did things together.

19

No one ever believed Mother was nearly fifty.

"We're more like sisters."

Umph, Lynn muttered to herself. Mother said she'd be a gay grandmother, but it didn't look as if she'd ever have a son-in-law if life continued on its pattern. It was odd how mother never thought any of Lynn's boy-friends a possible. Lynn knew she was influenced by her mother's opinion but at the same time she was aware that she'd never met a man that she felt was the man for her.

On Friday night she arrived home having rehearsed how she would break the news of her leaving Hendon's.

"Hallo, dear," Mother called. "What a day. It's nice and warm in here."

It had been snowing heavily but instead of being white the roads were grey and slushy and only here and there on foliage or in odd corners was there anything white.

Lynn shook the moisture off her dark hair and appreciated the wave of warm air that met her. Then she took off her coat and went into the lounge.

Mother was smiling. She wasn't like

Lynn in looks though they each had a slim figure and were about the same height, five foot three.

"Guess what I've done today." Lynn introduced the subject that was uppermost in her thoughts.

Mary Laurel raised her eyebrows. As she heard, her expression changed, to consternation and a sharpening of the interest in her eyes, then she relaxed and laughed softly. "This is a surprise."

"I felt I'd had enough there." In spite of herself Lynn spoke defensively.

"But I thought you liked the work?" Mary Laurel was trying to understand.

Lynn nodded but was silent. She couldn't explain.

"Well, you won't find it difficult to get another job. When do you leave?"

"A week today."

"Well . . ." Mother's mind was working fast, Lynn could see and began to breathe more easily now that the news was out. "If I were you I should . . ."

Lynn felt herself stiffen. Mother was preparing to take over her affairs.

"Don't bother to get a permanent job yet, not for the summer. Go to an agency and say you will have work by the week or the fortnight . . ."

Lynn found herself listening, hypnotised, then she made a laughing protest. "I've got to work. Anyway I've a job when I leave. I've told Mrs. Tracey I'll see if any more can be done to find her daughter. I've said I'll finish the case." Lynn never talked of her work at home but Mary Laurel realised sufficient to be pleased.

"What a good idea. You'll be able to work from home."

Lynn shut her eyes and saw she'd have to be firm with her mother in future—and herself.

At the office Lynn worked out her week. Now that she was leaving she found she had a different attitude to the place and her job—or was it to herself? Was she conscious of some unexpected self-respect?

Ellis was interested in his kindly way and reiterated the fact that he thought she was wise. "It's dull here for a bright girl like you. I expect you'll try and get a job in a large firm where they've a social and sports club?"

Lynn was vague.

Clive was curious. "I never thought you'd walk out on us."

Lynn raised her eyebrows and laughed inside. It wasn't often that Clive admitted to being stumped.

"I didn't think you had it in you."

She flared. "You don't know human nature."

His eyes flashed and his mouth snapped shut. She had hit him on a vulnerable point. If there was one thing on which Clive prided himself, it was his knowledge of human nature!

She swallowed a chuckle. She hadn't got to work with him in future so it didn't matter if she got his back up.

"You've probably always thought of me as part of the office furnishings," she pushed on. "I'm not."

He cleared his throat. "Thanks for the information. I'll file it."

She concentrated on her typing, aware that she was being upheld on a rising tide of excitement. She appeared to be behaving impetuously. She wasn't really. Mrs. Tracey's plea that she should continue privately with the case had been the spur she needed to make her act as she'd been dreaming of acting for over a year. For self-preservation she knew she had to break from her mother's possessiveness.

It wasn't a busy period at Hendon's so she had time to think round the Tracey business and the more she thought the more her sympathy was with Joan. She couldn't make up her mind if the girl had been frustrated to breaking point—or frightened. If she were frightened what was its cause? People who ran away often were frightened.

She stopped typing and stared straight ahead. Mrs. Tracey had offered her a high weekly wage plus expenses while she worked on the case but that wasn't Lynn's only reason for taking the job. She felt sympathetically in tune with Joan and instinctively felt she could help her.

Lynn dreamed of opening doors. After she had cleared up the Tracey case she might travel. Clive wasn't the only one who had the world as his oyster. It was hers as well as his.

She might go to New Zealand. There were some of her father's cousins living in the South Island. Mother had relatives in Canada but Lynn shied away from them.

One evening she made an appointment and went to the Traceys' from the office.

They lived in a large detached house that stood rather forbiddingly in its own grounds. Lynn walked slowly up the short drive and without consciously doing so photographed the house, Fircroft, on her mind. It was the firs that gave it a dark look, she thought, and rang the bell firmly keeping her thumb on it for a few seconds.

A plump, comfortably dressed woman opened the door and took her to Mrs. Tracey's "sanctum". The plump woman was Mr. Tracey's sister . . . and a natural human being, Lynn thought. Joan could have made a confidante of her.

"It is so good of you to come." Mrs. Tracey waved Lynn to a seat and sat forward with clasped hands, letting her sophisticated veneer slip. She was a distraught woman.

"I'm afraid I haven't any news," Lynn said. "I only came to tell you that I shan't be at the office after next Friday, but shall be working from home." She gave Mrs. Tracey a piece of card with her address,

25

and added comfortingly, "Then I shall have all the time there is."

Mrs. Tracey nodded slowly, and put the card in the drawer of a genuine Chippendale table. Mrs. Tracey's room was a show place. Every piece belonged.

The whole house was the same.

Lynn looked round Joan's bedroom. It was a neat room . . . and very dainty. The white furniture picked out in gold was none of that done-at-home stuff! The carpet was thick and pastel pink. The curtains toned, and the bedspread. In vain Lynn looked for any sign of Joan's personality . . . books, record player, snapshots poked into odd holders.

"It's just as she left it."

Lynn suppressed a shudder. Poor Joan.

She was leaving when Mr. Tracey arrived home. He was something in the City and drove a car that looked as if he must be something pretty big. There was no lack of money at Fircroft. She photographed the big fleshy man in her mind and thought with sympathy he was as much at a loss as his wife to explain Joan's disappearance.

"She could have had anything. We'd

just done up her bedroom. That furniture was all new last year."

Mr. Tracey's sister prepared to see Lynn out, "Vivian Tracey," she introduced herself. "Would you like a cup of tea before you go?"

Lynn nodded. Here was humanity at last. The Traceys were in some way behind a brick wall. Perhaps they'd done too much outstripping the Joneses to be quite real any longer with strangers?

"This business of Joan has broken their hearts," Vivian Tracey said abruptly. She had taken over the small room off the kitchen as a sitting room . . . and though the furniture was in period, Vivian Tracey wasn't, and neither were her knick-knacks. And she had picture postcards on the mantelpiece. They were bright with blue seas and blue skies. "It's Summer in those islands. I've worked there in a school for twenty years."

"Why did Joan leave home, Miss Tracey?" Lynn blurted out the question.

"I don't know. She had left before I got home. I'm only on leave."

Disappointed Lynn drank her tea.

"You know the saying, apple of one's eye? Joan was the apple of their eyes . . ."

She must have been tough, or driven, to go and leave so much hurt behind, Lynn thought.

"My heart aches—for all three of them," Vivian Tracey declared.

The following evening Lynn visited the hospital where Joan had worked. She had authority from the Traceys to make enquiries and was fortunate to find the receptionist on duty remembered Joan.

"She was a sweet girl, and so kind."

"Kind?" Lynn said.

"Yes, you know what I mean. She felt for people, for the patients. She used to visit one man who had no one to visit him."

Ah-h, Lynn thought. Not *cherchez la femme* but the man and asked a few, not too obvious, questions, but she learned little beyond the fact that the man had been transferred to another hospital—"for some plastic surgery I think it was. He'd been hurt in an accident."

Soon after his removal Joan had left.

Lynn left the hospital in a thoughtful mood. There was nothing so human on the

Hendon file, but she had learned it almost without seeking.

At the house where Joan had her London bed-sitter the housekeeper remembered her well. "A nice little thing, and quiet. That's more than we can say for some. They're young and they enjoy themselves." She frowned and lit a cigarette. "She wasn't a mixer, but she wasn't stand-offish. I always felt she had a very kind streak in her. She was . . ." the housekeeper sought for the right word ". . . compassionate. She seemed as if she wanted to understand people."

Lynn left the hospital and the house where Joan had stayed with a very different picture of Joan Tracey from what she had been forming. She was emerging as a human, compassionate woman, not a frustrated, emotional girl.

It was puzzling. The jig-saw did not fit at any point.

The cold damp weather continued. It must have been a few degrees warmer because the rain wasn't snow or sleet, but it didn't seem any less raw.

Lynn thought of the Traceys and their anxiety. At one time she had wondered if they were fundamentally cold people, more concerned with their good name than their daughter's welfare. Now she believed they were a truly worried mother and father.

She didn't think Fircroft could have been a homely home. She didn't believe there was much display of affection. But the two facts welded together and magnified weren't enough to drive out Joan.

What else was there in the file? During her lunch hour next day, after a quick snack in the café next door, she went through it.

She had just decided she had a note of all the gen, when Clive came in—unusual for him at this time. He was pretty regular with his lunch hour as he went to a club. She looked at him questioningly.

He looked at the file on her desk.

"I'm interested in it," she answered his unspoken question.

"Why? The case is closed."

"Perhaps I wanted some lunchtime reading as it's too cold to go wandering round the shop windows." She sat up and pulled the rainbow sweater up round her neck. "There's no reason why I shouldn't

30

read it, is there?" she asked and she knew her voice had a different tone from what it would have had a week ago. She was leaving Hendon's. Subconsciously she felt in a different relationship to Clive. He wouldn't be one of her bosses in a few days' time.

"Er . . . no," he answered and Lynn wasn't sure whether he was uncertain because there was something odd about the Tracey case, or because of her manner.

During that week, she had a letter from her father.

He wrote to her often if not regularly, and it was always a red-letter day when she heard from him. He was an unpredictable person and had a job that took him all over the world. This time he wrote from Edinburgh where he had his permanent home, and spoke of a young Australian colleague, Jack Delmore. "He's coming to London almost immediately partly for the firm, partly on holiday and I've suggested he calls on you and that you may be willing to show him some of the sights of the capital."

Lynn nodded to herself. Of course she'd be willing. She liked doing things to please

31

her father. He never promised anything in her name or made her feel she *ought* to do a thing. He had too much respect for her as a human being.

Politely he hoped Mary was well. Mother rarely mentioned Dad, and if she did there was an edge in her voice, but he was always amiable when he spoke of her. He was a tolerant man, but Lynn sympathised with her mother. She had never been able to understand Dad's leaving her. She had no idea to what extent she had tried to run his life, mould his ideas, choose his beliefs.

She told Mary about Jack Delmore.

Mary raised her nicely defined eyebrows and looked at Lynn. "I wonder what he will be like?" she said mildly, but from the tone of her voice Lynn gathered he was hardly likely to be Mr. Right.

He came on the Thursday of that week, having rung up late on Wednesday.

"What an accent!" Mother exclaimed as she handed the phone to Lynn.

Mother was right.

And the accent matched the man, Lynn decided. It was different from any English accent she knew. And Jack Delmore was different from any fellow she'd been out with.

He was of medium height, with medium colouring and nothing much to look at. He had light brown eyes and wore a light brown tweed suit. He was forthright and in a hurry.

"I'm over here on a short trip. Your dad said I might persuade you to take me around," he said on the phone. "Can I?"

Lynn hedged. "It's an idea."

"What's the meaning of that crack? Yes or no."

"Yes," Lynn swallowed. She was to find that he never played verbal ball. He arranged to meet her and was waiting outside the office when she left on Thursday evening. It was then that she had her first impression that never left her. He was brown, a warm brown.

They went out to a meal and talked. He told her about his life in Australia and she read between the lines that he was a pretty good mining engineer, not afraid of hard work.

"You're over here on holiday?"

"Yep. More or less. With the parents. They're staying with your dad for a few days then we're off to the Scandinavian countries." He was interested in some plant the Norwegian engineers were testing that her father had told him about. "The parents reckoned they'd done enough for a bit but I wanted to have a look round down here. They can stay on after I go back if the bug bites 'em."

Later they went to a theatre and then he took her home by taxi. "If I were staying I'd get a car, but the folk reckon they'll be taking-in Europe and I reckon I'll go along."

Her mother made him come in for a drink and was her usual charming, civilised self. When he'd gone she raised her eyebrows and looked amused. "Well?"

"I think he's rather nice," Lynn said.

"Different and so a pleasant change," agreed Mary. "When are you going to see him again?"

"He said he'd phone."

It was quite a week. On Friday the Hendon's took Lynn out to a farewell dinner. It was a foursome of Ellis and his wife Irene, Clive and Lynn, and they went to a special restaurant. "Reserved as a rule for Ellis's special clients," Clive told Lynn.

She declared herself impressed and caught Irene's amused eyes. When Lynn had been on holiday Irene had done her job at Hendon's in the past and she was going to take over again until the right receptionist/secretary could be found.

"I'm not kidding, Lynn, but they won't find it easy to replace you."

Clive made a "shucks" noise.

"You can be uppish, but you won't find me doing your work so good-temperedly as Lynn did," Irene warned him. "I'm not typing your post and getting it off the same night if you don't come in at a reasonable hour."

"Petticoat government," he muttered in one of his favourite phrases and there was no questioning his opinion of it.

"You'd be lost without us," Irene retorted and Lynn laughed. Irene always answered Clive back. Lynn couldn't be bothered—not often. She'd done so this week more than she'd ever done—because she was leaving, she supposed and wouldn't be subject to his often erratic hours. If it hadn't been for Ellis, his consideration and kindness and the good pay-packet Lynn didn't think she'd have stayed so long.

"Can you believe this is really the end of the road for you at Hendon's?" Irene interrupted her thoughts.

"No," Lynn shook her head. She couldn't believe that next Monday she wouldn't have to catch the 8.27 bus from the corner.

"Ellis tells me you haven't a job to go to . . ."

Lynn was about to say that was right when Ellis touched his wife's hand and warned her. "Don't try and persuade Lynn to change her mind. That wouldn't be fair. You're not to play on her good nature—we've done that too much in the past. Let the girl go and have some fun in her next job."

"Fun," Clive groaned. "Is that what the measure of a job has become, fun?"

"No, but most firms can offer more than we can. We've no social club. We'd nothing to offer Lynn in the evenings . . ."

"I'd have taken her to the pictures," Clive's aggrieved voice touched off their laughter and it was a hilarious meal in a friendly unsophisticated way.

They had their coffee in a lounge and while they were in the powder room Irene said to Lynn, "They will miss you. Ellis knows it. Clive has to learn that truth."

Lynn chuckled. She liked Clive but she had never felt at ease with him as she did with Ellis. He was too sure of himself, too interested in himself—and not her? Lynn shrugged and admitted that was probably the truth.

"I hope you'll keep in touch with us and let us know how you make out," Irene continued.

"I will," Lynn said and imagined mailing cards from the other ends of the world once she had traced Joan Tracey. She found she wasn't thinking in terms of restoring her to her parents, but of finding her and letting her take the decision about a return home.

Over coffee Lynn was presented with her leaving presents.

"Oh-h," she gasped, momentarily over-whelmed as she examined the handbag and travelling case. "Thank you all so much."

"Thank them, not me," Clive

commanded gruffly, and just as Lynn felt herself flushing and her pleasure evaporating he thrust a small package into her hands.

It was a bright star-shaped brooch that seemed to sparkle with every colour. She caught her breath and then thanked him almost formally, but her eyes were aglow and the animation lit up her face, and her fingers fumbled as she tried to fasten it on the shoulder of her frock.

"Let me," he grunted and though not adept he did make a better job than she did.

Later he took her home. "Moonlight and icicles," he grinned. "Sorry I couldn't make it moonlight and roses, but if you will leave in such weather . . ." He shivered exaggeratedly and looked down at her.

For a moment she stood looking up. This was goodbye. There had never been anything between them specially but she had always been aware of him and something in him that antagonised the feminine in her. It was his masculine superiority probably.

He wouldn't come in, so they shook

hands and then, lightly, he kissed her cheek. "Amazing," he murmured mockingly. "I've known you for five years and we've never kissed."

"I hope you are more attracted by your next secretary," she laughed, unmoved. She had never wanted to kiss him or to be kissed by him . . . but she did wonder what a real kiss would be like.

Nevertheless as she walked up to the first floor and opened the door of Number 5 her thoughts had switched and she was thinking of Jack Delmore.

3

LYNN entered the new phase of her life with a feeling of expectancy and a sense of achievement. She had done something about her life at last! It wasn't what she'd dreamed. She hadn't broken away from home, she hadn't gained her freedom, but no one knew what this leaving Hendon's might lead to.

She went over the case methodically, listing the new information she had learned during the last week and pondering on the emerging picture. It was different from the one on the office files, but that didn't mean it would be easier to solve.

Lynn sat at the desk in her bed-sitter at home and allowed herself to dream. This might well be the beginning of work along the lines of this present job. She might become a "Hendon's" herself! If she solved this case successfully . . .

Lynn pursed her lips and her hazel eyes were thoughtful as she found her sympathy for Joan Tracey growing. She sounded a nice girl, and kind. Then what could have made her treat her parents so unkindly?

It had never become a newspaper case. Lynn, because of her job, could remember many cases of missing persons that had been reported and knew the Traceys had been at pains to avoid publicity. It was to be kept that way. Lynn imagined the Traceys kept up a façade to their friends and neighbours.

"Phone, Lynn," her mother called on that first morning of her being self-employed and asked with a chuckle, "Do I ask who's calling and then say you're busy and will the caller ring back?"

Lynn laughed and picked up the phone. It was Jack Delmore. As she imagined his rather square tanned face and mid-brown eyes her voice took on a lilt. "Hello, Jack."

He came to the point. "The parents are off to Norway this week, on Wednesday, so I was wondering if you could show me a few more sights of London?"

"Yes . . . I'd like to." She had learned

from their one meeting that he didn't fall into verbal shuttlecocks.

"Would Tuesday suit you?"

"Fine."

"Grand. Shall I call for you?" He knew she had left the office so arranged to pick her up at six o'clock at home.

Lynn put down the phone with a smile playing round her lips and her eyes dancing. Tuesday. Tomorrow. Not long to wait. "That was Jack Delmore," she told her mother unnecessarily.

Mary Laurel laughed. "I couldn't have mistaken the accent. I suppose he wants to get in all he can during a short stay."

Mother wasn't exactly asking for information, so Lynn didn't give her any. She said simply, "Yes, I suppose so."

She felt her mother look at her but she was turning into her room where the Tracey file was waiting her attention. Imperceptibly her will was hardening. She wasn't ready to share anything about Jack.

The first half of February had been colder than average but in the second half the weather grew less severe though by no means warm, and Lynn looked out of the window at the leafless trees and black soil with the few green shoots breaking through and appreciated not having to wait for a bus at a draughty corner.

She appreciated working at home. Mary was good and left her to it, making just the right amount of fuss so that Lynn enjoyed the spoiling.

They went for a walk when Lynn had finished her "post", early in the afternoon. She had written an official thank you to Ellis and Irene Hendon, one to Clive and she had written for a booking to a hotel in North Faldon, the town where Joan Tracey had been living before she disappeared.

"This is most businesslike," smiled mother and insisted on their going for a walk round the park. "You must have some exercise. We'll come again tomorrow."

Lynn didn't answer, but felt a wariness creeping over her. Mother was very sweet, and considerate but—and it was a big but that was in Lynn's mind. Nothing must become a habit. She must not let herself become tied.

Luckily Mother often played bridge in the afternoons and she herself would be going away on Wednesday. Her mind went to the journey and she decided that she'd go to the library and get out a guide on the North Faldon district.

She read about the industrial town but knew it wouldn't come alive for her until she stepped out at the station. She was not one of those people who can read a guide-book and project themselves into the place.

The facet she found most puzzling about the Tracey case was Clive's behaviour. She could not find a satisfactory explanation as to why he gave it up. She would have said it was completely contrary to his nature to do so. He had limitless patience for dead-end cases. Yet he had written "finis" to this one while Lynn felt there were avenues still unexplored.

Was this due to some flaw in his character? Had he some feeling that he wouldn't be able to solve it so had written it off? Had he decided to close it so that he wouldn't have to admit defeat? Lynn admitted that the explanation didn't satisfy her. She chuckled even as she frowned over the point. It hurt her pride. She thought she knew Clive better than that.

After all, she had worked for Hendon's for five years, and she would have said that under his gay manner and often seeming inconsequence he had a tenacious streak that wasn't turned aside until nothing further could be done.

As a flash, a thought came to her but she didn't consider it seriously. Clive could be personally involved with Joan Tracey. Perhaps he had found her and was keeping quiet at her request?

Even while she shook her head Lynn had to admit that it was a remote possibility. People were so often different from what they seemed. The self they showed the world was rather like the iceberg above water, a very small part of the whole. If she judged other people by herself Lynn saw she would have to admit that they could be very different from their "social" self. She was. She didn't suppose anyone knew of her inner restlessness and urge for freedom.

Joan Tracey was very different from the girl put forward by her parents. Lynn remembered her talks with Mrs. Tracey, then with Vivian Tracey, the housekeeper and the receptionist.

Joan, to those who had met her after she had left home, had been friendly though quiet, kind and compassionate and not in the least frustrated or "difficult".

When she packed up "work" for the day on Tuesday Lynn was pleased with herself, experiencing a satisfied glow inside her. She had received confirmation over the phone of her booking at the Royal Hotel at North Faldon and she had her tickets for the journey. What a day's work, she grinned at her feeling of self-importance but didn't deny her excitement in being on her own if only for one case.

She dressed carefully for her outing with Jack, wearing a vivid frock of many greens. Mother had shaded her eyes at first sight of it, but Lynn believed it suited her.

The frock was high-necked. Often Lynn wore special beads but today she hesitated and finally pinned Clive's brooch to one side, and a smile broke over her face as she nodded. It was right.

Jack obviously thought so, too. At any rate he noticed it when she took off her coat as they sat down to dinner and remarked on it.

"You look swell," he said in his blunt way.

He looked his usual light brown, warm self, although he was wearing a lightweight suit not a tweed.

"I like that—er—thing on your frock. It looks super. I reckon it's not part of the outfit."

"No," Lynn admitted. "It was a present."

"Guessed it must have been. Um . . ." He consulted her and ordered dinner, then his mind went back to the brooch. Looking at it he said, "Your Dad said you hadn't a permanent boy-friend."

"Oh did he?" Lynn smiled.

"Does that mean you have?" Jack asked in his plain-spoken way. He'd no finesse.

"No." Lynn couldn't string him along. He'd take all she said literally.

"But I guess you've got plenty of casuals."

Lynn nodded. She had. They came— and they went.

He nodded, asked if the soup was to her liking and then continued. "We've got to settle down one day. I never thought much about it when I was getting on with the

47

job of establishing myself. Now . . ." He talked of his prospects and ambitions. He knew where he was going. "So I reckon it's time I relaxed a bit and had a look round."

"You're going to Europe with your parents, aren't you?"

"'Sright. I'm off to Norway tomorrow —partly business."

He told her of the mining plant he had an appointment to view. "But I'll be back." His eyes met hers and he didn't have to say any more.

Lynn was glad. She liked Jack Delmore.

Her mother was her usual, charming self and insisted on his staying to coffee when he brought Lynn home. "You must. You are Lynn's friend and I haven't been given the chance to say more than 'hallo' to you yet."

"No," he agreed literally. "But I'll be back after the Norway trip."

He accepted Mary Laurel without any reactions as far as Lynn could observe and her heart lifted. Most young men seemed to become wary when they met her mother.

Jack Delmore was unselfconsciously

himself. He talked of Lynn's father and obviously thought a lot of him. "Lynn's like him, isn't she?"

Mary looked at her daughter and laughed quietly, helplessly.

Lynn knew what she was thinking. Here was a very odd young man, not at all suitable as a son-in-law.

Next day when Jack was flying to Norway Lynn took the inter-city train to North Faldon. She had a notebook, a couple of pens and a woman's magazine that she read most of the way until they were coming near to her destination.

North Faldon station was in the centre of the town. Lynn looked round taking in the new civic centre which was dominated by a modern Town Hall. From her reading she knew there was a church of cathedral proportions in the old section of the town and, on the outskirts a big prison.

Her first impression was that it was a cold bustling place—the wind from the east had a sting in it, and she wondered what on earth had made Joan Tracey choose to live here. She wasn't surprised she'd left it!

Her hotel was central and warm, and the

hall welcomed her with a bowl of golden daffodils on the polished table. It had been a coaching inn and still had the welcoming atmosphere that must have been extended to travellers for generations.

Lynn signed at the Reception and gave herself a shake. This was her first job on her own. Her spirits rose and she was aware of a simmering excitement that was to stay with her throughout the visit.

Her first line of enquiry was to visit the address that Joan Tracey had given her parents and from which she had written so regularly at first and which they had visited. Clive had covered this ground, of course, and Lynn had read his reports but she had deliberately put out of her mind what she had learned, or at any rate pushed it into her subconscious and was going forward with an empty and receptive mind.

Joan's landlady was a business woman. She remembered Joan. "I'm sorry she's still missing. Loss of memory I reckon. She was a quiet girl. I can't let you see her room as I've re-let it and I don't hold with going into tenant's rooms. But she didn't leave anything behind except one of her Spanish books."

Lynn blinked, "Spanish?"

"She was learning Spanish, at night school. She seemed dead set on it, too. You know what I mean, studied it seriously. She didn't just play at it."

"No . . ."

"She was the serious type—but she wasn't dull. In fact the week before she left she was quite excited for her."

"She gave you notice then? She didn't just walk out?"

"Of course she didn't. She wasn't that sort. She was a thoroughly nice girl and I couldn't have wished for a better lodger. I told her mother so and the young man who came up here enquiring . . . It's funny I must say she hasn't written home, but that's her business. She was all right by me."

"Did you tell the young man about the Spanish?"

"Course I did. That was the only thing I could tell him that was in any ways unusual."

"Ye-es." Lynn talked on casually for a few minutes and then left. She had learned one very odd fact. Clive had known about Joan's learning Spanish but he had never entered it on her file. Lynn was sure of that. She had read the file too often to have missed it.

After she left the house she went back. "Sorry to bother you, but have you got that Spanish book of Miss Tracey's?"

"No, I gave it to the young man. I do hope nothing's happened to her. I shouldn't like to think of anything doing that."

Lynn's simmering excitement bubbled. What was Clive's game?

The landlady had suggested that Lynn should go to the shop on the corner where Joan used to do most of her shopping. "She cooked for herself and thank 'eavens she wasn't one to go in for smells. I never did smell a kipper or an onion while she was with me."

Joan had done a part-time job at the hospital as she had done down South, but this time she hadn't visited any of the patients.

The shopkeeper remembered her vaguely. "Yes, she used to come in here, but it was the wife who used to serve her

52

most often." His wife was away visiting a married daughter who was going to have her second. Lynn heard quite a bit of the family history, then the man remembered Mrs. Wilson. "She does for us and she's doing extra for me with the missus away. She's not there now. She went afore dinner. But she used to do for the Tracey lass."

Lynn visited her later that afternoon and found her in a small council house built specially for singles. "Not so bad, is it?" she asked after telling Lynn to sit down and putting on the kettle. "It's not so cheap as the place the council pulled down, but that's these councils . . ."

Lynn judged that Mrs. Wilson liked money. Miss Tracey's had helped. But she also gathered that Mrs. Wilson had genuinely liked Joan, it wasn't only the bit extra.

Lynn knew Joan's financial position. She had never been short of money, and had continued to receive her allowance from home after she left and had taken the first hospital job. The account had been transferred to North Faldon, and then when Joan left it had been closed, not transferred.

Mrs. Wilson gave her a cup of tea and looked at her suspiciously. "You're another of 'em."

Lynn nodded. "Her mother is anxious about her."

"Humph. That's what the young fellow said. But the mother didn't come and see me."

"She wouldn't be making this effort to find her if she wasn't though, would she?"

"S'pose not." Mrs. Wilson took a mouthful of tea and held it in her mouth as if savouring it before she swallowed. "Don't know nothing about that. Don't know nothing about you, either. Why are you snooping?"

"I told you, her mother is anxious to know that she is all right."

"She is. She's a good girl."

"Her mother will be relieved to know she's not ill," Lynn said and controlled her urge to try and make Mrs. Wilson get on with it. It was obvious Mrs. Wilson had information.

"Kind and generous, too. When I did any shopping for her she always used to tell me to get a tin of something for me supper."

There followed a wandering series of memories about trivialities that did little more than confirm that Joan Tracey was a generous girl with a mind of her own, but out of the welter Lynn gradually found she was getting something more. She realised Mrs. Wilson knew where Joan was.

"She told me where she was going but nobody else. She knew I wouldn't tell nobody."

Lynn marvelled. She'd never have expected anyone like Mrs. Wilson to have kept silent. Had Joan paid her well? She dismissed the idea. She didn't think so. She was listening to a list of Joan's dislikes from the greengrocer's when she heard something that made her sit up. "So I took her some of his bananas when I went to see her. She always did say his were the best bananas she'd ever tasted."

"She liked bananas then?" Lynn asked automatically, scarcely aware of what she was saying. So Mrs. Wilson had been to see Joan? Here was a real break at last.

She kept silent while Mrs. Wilson confirmed the banana tale, seeking in her mind how she could get the information of Joan's whereabouts. Presently she talked about Joan's learning Spanish. "I understand she went to night school."

"Yep." Mrs. Wilson knew all about it.

"I wonder if she was good at languages?"

"I wouldn't know. Double Dutch to me. She showed me some of the words and I laughed in her face. Not for me, ducks. Give me the good old English lingo that makes plain sense."

"But she went on learning it?"

"Yep."

Lynn drew a deep breath. This wasn't getting her anywhere. "I wonder . . ." she began and felt like crossing her fingers so that she might word her request appealingly, "I wonder, Mrs. Wilson," she said boldly starting again, "if you would take me to see Joan Tracey?"

"I can't, duck." Mrs. Wilson's voice was triumphant.

"Please. I'll promise not to do anything against her wishes when I've seen her."

Mrs. Wilson shook her head.

"But . . ."

The woman stopped her pleading. "I

can't. She's not anywhere near now. Look at this." She took a postcard from her handbag and held it out to Lynn.

It was a card of a beach in the South of Spain.

"Flavidest." Lynn read and looked at Mrs. Wilson.

"Come two days ago," Mrs. Wilson beamed. "See what she says . . . about flying there and arriving safely and finding it 'ot and sunny."

Lynn read. "She hasn't signed it."

"But it's her 'and-writing."

4

LYNN stared at Mrs. Wilson as she assimilated this information regarding Joan Tracey. She was in Spain, at a place called Flavidest. Lynn had never heard of it but from the card saw that it had a harbour, a blue sky and a deeper blue sea. The card was, presumably showing the view from a height above the harbour so that the rocky wave-swept coast was spread out and away from land there was an island.

Lynn handed back the card. "It looks very nice," she said lamely and looked out of the window at the watery February sunlight. This was unexpected. "You're sure it's Joan's handwriting?"

"Course it is. Bless you, I used to post enough letters from her to him when she was studying that there Spanish and didn't want to go out."

Letters to him. Lynn's mind registered the fact but she didn't blink an eyelash— she hoped. "It must be marvellous to go

58

to a Mediterranean country at this time of the year. What made—them decide on Spain?"

"Blessed if I know. I never heard her say, but I daresay it was his idea."

"Y-e-es." Here was food for thought. She had almost forgotten the man whom Joan visited in the London hospital because he had no one else. Then he had been transferred to another hospital the receptionist had told her. Had he come to North Faldon? If he had, it hadn't presumably been to a hospital or there'd have been some report of Joan's going hospital visiting. Probably . . . Lynn's mind fastened on a fact she'd overlooked. Joan used to write to him so he wasn't in North Faldon. Then why on earth had she come up here? If she wanted to learn Spanish there were hundreds of schools in the South.

There were dozens of loose threads but Lynn felt there was some justification for connecting the man in hospital with the man with whom Joan had gone to Spain. Two and two seemed to make four.

A warning rang in her mind. She hadn't worked for Hendon's without knowing how easy it is to make events fit a situation.

"I suppose you won't be writing to her?" Lynn asked, more for something to say than because she expected a helpful answer.

"Bless you no. What'd I have to tell her and what sort of a picture would she want from Faldon?"

Lynn shook her head laughing, then she thanked Mrs. Wilson for her help and asked suddenly, "What's her boy friend's name?"

"Dunno as I can remember," Mrs. Wilson shook her head.

Yet she had posted letters to him often enough, Lynn thought as she left the house, and she admired Mrs. Wilson's loyalty. It was a nuisance from her own point of view but it meant Mrs. Wilson had truly liked Joan. But why couldn't the name be given?

Going home in the train Lynn pondered on that odd facet. It held her attention although it was only one of many. The other most puzzling feature was why had Clive hidden the fact that Joan was learning Spanish.

Lynn's mind went round in circles but when she arrived home she hadn't had a glimmer of light. There was a card from Jack, from Norway. Her face lit up and she pushed the case to the back of her mind as she read his bold, easy to decipher writing. He had arrived safely after a good flight and was impressed with the plant that he had visited yesterday. The Norwegian engineers were developing this process in a big way.

Lynn chuckled to herself. It was almost as fogging to her as the case! But she put his card on her desk and was very pleased that he had thought about her.

Later that evening there was a phone call from her father. Her mother had gone to an Oxfam committee meeting so Lynn was alone.

"What's going on?" he asked. "I phoned Hendon's and was told you'd left. What are you doing?"

"I meant to write and tell you." Lynn bit her lip remorsefully. She'd quite forgotten. "Where are you?" It wasn't a long distance call.

"At the Maydown." That was his club

61

in London. "Good." Lynn's voice rose in quick pleasure. "When shall I see you?"

"Well . . ." Lynn imagined him turning up his diary though she knew he had the possible dates and times already fixed in his mind. That was Dad all over. He never rushed anybody or appeared to be bullying. It was one of the reasons why he had been so successful in his job, she thought, and made a mental note to follow his example where she could. "What can you manage? Have you any free evenings this week? What about tomorrow?"

So tomorrow it was. Lynn dressed carefully, pinning Clive's brooch to her frock. It wasn't the multi-green dress but a dull red and the brooch seemed made for it as it had the green. The red frock went with her red coat.

Her father raised his eyebrows approvingly and made the motions of a wolf whistle, much as Clive had done. It was the first time he had seen the coat.

She chuckled happily. Over dinner at his club they talked and went on talking in the lounge over coffee later. He wanted to hear all about Hendon's and what she was ready to tell him of the job she'd undertaken for the Traceys. He looked at her consideringly.

"Your heart's in it. You want to find that girl. You want to help her."

Lynn nodded.

"You're doing a good job but . . ."

Lynn waited and as she expected out came a typical Dad's remark.

". . . don't nag her into doing anything because it seems the right thing to do. She must decide . . ." His eyes looked levelly into hers. "Your job is limited." He picked up the thought she had already had and underlined it. "You have to set Mrs. Tracey's mind at rest. You don't have to make her daughter return to the parental nest."

Lynn had already decided that but she was glad of this confirmation of her own feelings. She told him she was going to Spain.

"Where are you staying?"

Lynn looked at her agency reservations. "Hotel Miranda, Flavidest."

He knew that part of Spain and gave her a happy picture.

Presently he talked about the Delmores.

"I hear you've been taking young Jack around."

"I've been showing him London . . . but I can't say we've seen much."

Her father laughed. "I don't suppose that's worried him. He's a nice fellow—don't you think so?"

"Yes."

"They're a nice family. When they come back from touring you must come to Edinburgh and get to know them. Would you like that?"

Lynn's eyes lit up. "I'll give myself a week's leave."

"Splendid."

They didn't talk of the details of the Tracey case; to Lynn that wouldn't have been right, but her father's general observations and his approval that she was doing a good job were a spur when she was sitting at her desk next morning working out the next step.

Reading between the lines she also thought he had hinted it wouldn't be a bad idea if she left home for a while . . . stepped out. Well, she was going to step out to Spain.

She made her wardrobe preparations in a holiday mood, helped by mother.

"It will be warm out there, I know the temperature even at this time of the year is in the sixties. But you must take some warm clothes. I'm sure it can be chilly in the evenings. It might be quite a notion if you look round while you're there and fixed up for a holiday for us later in the year. What do you think of the idea?"

Lynn shied away from it, but she hadn't the courage to say so. "It is an idea," she agreed. "But I imagine Flavidest is only a small fishing village, though that coast is developing into a holiday playground."

"You must take your bathing gear, and sun bathing frocks . . ."

"I'm going there to work," Lynn protested. "I may not be there more than a few days."

"When you've done the job you could stay on. I might fly out and join you."

It was another idea, one that Lynn knew her mother was capable of translating into action.

She wanted to protest, to beg to be left alone, but her love for her mother pushed the feelings aside and she knew sympathy.

Mother hadn't had any real holidays for years . . . not as her colleagues had. Devoting herself to Lynn she had been limited by Lynn's likes and wants.

"Thanks for your help in getting me ready," she burst out.

She had arranged with the travel agency to get her air ticket to Alicante leaving open the return date, and to arrange currency and her traveller's cheques. To Flavidest, that was little known as a tourist resort yet, she would have to go by car. The agency arranged that for her. "You will be met," the clerk told her and added with a smile, "or if you are not, the car will turn up sometime. They are a delightfully haphazard people as regards time in that part. Tomorrow will do."

Lynn raised her eyebrows and laughed at herself. She was inclined to think the same unless she drove herself to a decision.

She phoned Mrs. Tracey and called the following afternoon. As she sat with her Lynn felt again the lack of homeliness in Fircroft and tried to imagine Joan's living there.

"I'm sure she is well, Mrs. Tracey," Lynn said but had no comforting answers

66

to "Why is she treating us like this? What have we done to deserve it?"

That was a trait in Joan's character for which Lynn had no answer or theory. It seemed to contradict what she had learned of the girl's kind nature.

She had little to tell Mrs. Tracey. She didn't think the time was opportune to say there might be a man involved. She had come for some photos of Joan so that she should have a good chance of recognising her if she ran into her, as she hoped to do, in Flavidest. She wasn't likely to be travelling under her own name. She had used it at North Faldon, but she had still been in touch with her parents then.

Lynn looked at the photos and snaps. Joan Tracey was tall, with fairish thick hair that she wore quite short. "That's how it was when I last saw her."

Mrs. Tracey looked at the snap and her eyes filled with tears.

The hair could have been grown, Lynn realised or have been cut shorter. But the eyes would be the same, set wide apart and big. "They're a beautiful brown . . ."

And the mouth wouldn't have altered. Lynn looked at several photos and snaps, taken recently and during the past ten years. Joan had a round, plumpish face in them all, but the chin was a determined feature. Her nose was straight and suited her face. It was the mouth and chin that gave her character.

Next day Lynn took off for Spain, feeling free and unfettered, a feeling that increased once the plane was airborne.

The world was her oyster. Clive wasn't the only one who had such a world. She had, too.

Her hand went to the lapel of her coat, a mixture weave of reds and blues. His brooch went there as well as it did on her frocks.

They left England amid outbursts of snow or sleet. Soon they were above the clouds in sunshine and when they landed at Alicante it was in clear bright weather and an atmosphere that embraced you warmly. And the date was the 8th of March! Lynn smiled incredulously and appreciatively.

As the customs' formalities were completed she thought how amazing it was that she was here on a job. Both Ellis and Clive had often been abroad for the firm, but she had only had the joy of typing their reports—and they never mentioned the weather! Last winter Clive had gone to Tunisia but he'd never mentioned how blue the sea had looked or what flowers were in bloom. Lynn looked round and saw some climbing pink geraniums.

Her taxi had not arrived but she felt no sense of irritation. It was pleasant waiting in the sun. She had a suitcase on the dusty ground beside her and a large handbag that was nearly a holdall with all her personal papers and the necessary papers about the case.

She murmured over to herself the few Spanish words she had learned. If she was going in for this sort of work, becoming an agency in her own name, she'd have to swot at languages. Her French was good, so was her German, but she knew little Italian and no Spanish except . . . bano for bath, libros books.

She was going over some dozen words when a taxi swung into the gritty area in front of her and a young man jumped out of the driving seat almost before he'd stopped the car.

"I am Guan," he bowed. "How do you do?"

He picked up her case, put it in the back of the car and opened the door of the seat next to the driver. "Si."

She began speaking in English. He smiled and nodded but she soon realised his English was limited. During the ride to Flavidest they spoke in French of which he knew a little but it wasn't an enlightening ride though it was enjoyable. Guan was slim about her own height, with a dark skin and white teeth and light lively eyes that were very expressive and she had no doubt he approved of her looks.

She learned that he was a guide as well as a taxi and bus driver. "I speak all the languages," he declared. "But not the very much. How are you?"

"How are you" was his favourite English phrase and though a question, required no answer. When Lynn did begin to tell him he looked blank and could only smile.

She noticed the brown country through which they were driving, with its bare soil broken by patches of scrub, a few trees and some bushes. It was gouged with cracks and small crevices. It looks like cowboy country, Lynn thought and could imagine the sheriff's posse galloping after the Bad Man. Gulleys, dried up streams, volcanic boulders were features of the landscape with here and there orchards of citrus fruits, almond and olives.

It was an hour and a half's ride and though she enjoyed it Lynn was glad to look down from the top of a hill and across a wide bay, "Flavidest."

Guan stopped the car while she looked and nodded as she saw the island, rather a Gibraltar shaped rock, lying off from a cluster of houses round a small harbour. From this distance and height the place looked miniature.

"How far is the island?" she asked and even when she translated into French Guan shrugged and from his reply she gathered that it was only in the Summer that visitors were taken across.

He drove more swiftly now, down the winding road that led to the harbour and drew up with a screeching of brakes before the Hotel Miranda. It was a friendly family hotel where the proprietor, Pedro, could speak reasonably good English. There were tables on the terrace above the pavement outside and a café bar with restaurant inside. Through a glass door at the back Lynn was led to the "hotel" which seemed to be a lounge out of which the stairs ran to the bedrooms. She had a pleasant room at the side, with a balcony overlooking the harbour and a little removed from the outside section of the café where there were a few tables occupied—by locals she had judged after a quick glance on her way in. She had a photographic memory and examined her impressions when she was alone in her room, standing by the open window looking out over the sea. It was hard to believe it was March and that she had left England in a flurry of snow. She took off her coat and watched the waves running up this rocky side of the harbour and breaking into bursts of spray.

After she had looked her fill, though she thought it would be a long time before she got tired of watching the life that milled round, she unpacked a few of her things. She didn't want to get too settled, as if she were staying for a week. She might find

Joan Tracey immediately and be able to return right away.

Her first, and possibly her only, task was to locate Joan and talk to her. From the window she looked round the little town, village rather, and thought the task of finding an English woman shouldn't be too difficult.

What about the man that was—presumably—with her? Lynn admitted that she didn't know there was a man in the case but she felt pretty certain there must be.

Joan Tracey had rich parents. She was an only child. Was the man a fortune hunter? If he were, that wasn't really Lynn's business. All she had to do was to find Joan Tracey. Circumstances would dictate her next step.

Next morning she began her work in earnest. She made enquiries at the Miranda but no one had any information with regard to an English visitor, "Not one in particular, you understand," Pedro told her. "We have not many in the Winter but we always have the few and they come and they go."

Lynn took her first walk round Flavidest directly after breakfast, before the sun was clear of the mountains to the East, but she was warm enough with a cardigan slung over her shoulders. She looked at everything, taking in the busy harbour where the fishing boats came in with the catch every evening and auctioned it on the quay, at the cafés on the water-front, the statues to heroes of the liber-ation, the date palms with their clusters of fruit, the "English" flowers that belonged to May and June—blue and white iris, wallflowers, red, pink and puce climbing geraniums together with bougainvillaea, tamarisk-type bushes, lavender and sage, fading poinsettias.

She let her first impressions sink in, knowing they would be modified later. They must be superficial at first. Flavidest appeared to be far more a fishing village in the midst of a fruit growing district than a tourist centre. It was rather one of those artist villages that are still undisdovered by the public.

Lynn felt her description was inad-equate as she watched the people while she had an early mid-morning coffee. Her companions were locals, discussing the last night's football as far as she could guess and in no hurry to get anywhere or do anything. She felt at one with them in that. It would be easy to sit lazily in the sun, go in to a late lunch and sink into a siesta all the afternoon.

A man and a woman, obviously English, had coffee at the next table but the woman wasn't Joan Tracey. Lynn had no need to study any of the photos she had brought.

She looked at them carefully in the somnolence of the afternoon when the village was asleep. You could feel the warm quiet; Lynn succumbed to it for a quarter of an hour as her eyes became heavy and she dropped off. She was sitting on her bedroom balcony and the sun glinting on the water throwing back reflections, made sunglasses a must.

If Joan was staying in Flavidest Lynn felt sure she would run into her some time. There were a few apartments that were let to the winter visitors as well as a few hotels of the Miranda class and two that catered for a more sophisticated and luxury-loving clientele. Pedro had told her they were almost empty. His family were friendly and would have been helpful, Lynn thought, but there was the handicap of the language. She had brought a Spanish dictionary and thumbed through it when she was awake during the afternoon.

Now she was here, a thought came to her. Supposing she did not locate Joan? Supposing that card had been a red herring? It was possible she had put two and one together to make them add up to four.

Lynn took a realistic view without letting it get her down. In spite of the lack of proof she believed that card was from Joan, but she need only have been passing through the village.

After dinner, over which she took nearly two hours—as Pedro asked, "What is the hurry?"—she continued to sit outside. There were a few red roses in bloom up the far wall, with some white jasmine entwined. Two locals were talking to Pedro while the wireless played light music interspersed with talking that silenced Pedro and his companions, sometimes making them laugh, sometimes causing them to shake their heads. Lynn wondered if it were news or the results of sporting events. Whatever it was it never stopped the laughter and talking for long.

A car drew up at the curb and Pedro went to meet the man who was paying the driver, and picked up his bag.

"You have a room for me?" the man asked and Lynn jumped.

It was Clive's voice! She stared and recognised the walk. Sure enough the man was Clive Hendon.

5

LYNN felt so shocked that for a few moments her brain ceased to work. Clive Hendon here in Flavidest?

There was no mistake. It wasn't his double. It was Clive Hendon walking in his characteristically nonchalant way, wearing his usual colourful, casual clothes. His jacket and trousers were well cut, he even had a tailored appearance, but he didn't look conventional . . .

Lynn pulled herself together. She wasn't writing a description of Clive Hendon for the file of a new case. He was here. Why?

Her hazel eyes were dark as she concentrated. Naturally she assumed it was in connection with Joan Tracey. It would be too much of a coincidence to think otherwise. That meant the case wasn't closed! Unless . . . Lynn's mind travelled from point to point. Clive could have come out here following Joan for personal reasons. That could have been why he had dropped the case, because of a personal relationship with her. He could be the man in the case.

It was a shaking thought, but explained the odd facets of the business.

Where did Hendon's stand in this? Lynn's mind wandered because she wasn't happy in this development and she shied from continuing her thought process. She had heard from Irene Hendon before she left London. "We haven't been able to fill your place," she wrote. "We've had several applicants, satisfactory on paper, but Clive is too fussy. None suits his lordship. You spoilt him. He really did appreciate you, you know, although you said he didn't."

Lynn wrinkled her nose. She supposed Irene was right. Clive had appreciated her work—at least he had never really criticised it adversely. He'd often pulled her leg ... Lynn's smile widened. She supposed she hadn't responded. She'd always liked Ellis better than Clive. Privately she considered Clive a show-off and his "friendly" self patronising.

She forced her mind back to the case. If Clive was here with Joan what did she report to Mrs. Tracey? Their being together wasn't any of her business.

Questions, often irrelevant because she was so staggered at the development, tumbled about in her mind.

Did she stay or go?

She sat up straight, her eyes bright. Before she answered her own questions it would be interesting to hear what Clive had to say.

She had watched him go through the door from the restaurant into the reception lounge. Half the double door from the restaurant to the hotel was open, as usual, so she would watch. She saw him sign and then go upstairs with Pedro.

Lynn smiled to herself as she picked up her coffee cup and walked through the bar to the lounge and took a seat where she could see the stairs and would be able to see him immediately he began to come down.

It was a pleasantly comfortable lounge, well lit with modern furniture and bright yellow and green cushions scattered on the chairs and settees.

Lynn picked up a magazine and looked at the pictures—it was a Spanish periodical—but she wasn't really giving them her attention. Her mind was on Clive.

At the same time she realised she was alert. It was as if his surprise coming had sharpened her senses and she was ready for anything. She became aware of a man in the café on the other side of the hotel door. He was lolling back at a table, with his face and shoulders almost in the shade as the table lamp threw his pink shirt into bright relief. She couldn't see his eyes, but she knew he was watching her.

Her hand went to the brooch on the shoulder of her frock. It was Clive's star and showed up glitteringly on her dark green frock. With the cardigan hanging back off her shoulders she realised it probably caught the light, and wondered if the man had ideas. Her money was in her handbag, and her papers. There was no jewellery in her case upstairs but the brooch might give the impression that she had jewellery.

Lynn had been looking at the magazine while she wondered and putting it down abruptly looked at the man directly. He was still looking her way.

She heard a movement on the stairs and

saw Pedro returning. He stopped by her chair and enquired after her well-being. "We look after you the very good?"

"Very good indeed," she smiled.

"That is so. I get you some more coffee or the other drink?"

"Not just now, presently perhaps." She and Clive would probably have a drink together while she heard his tale.

She heard his footstep and looked up, tensing with quick excitement. He was going to be shaken.

He came slowly, hands in pockets, looking round and taking most interest in the small reception desk with the phone and the door leading to the café. As his eyes turned and searched her section of the lounge she spoke.

"Hallo, Clive." She noticed her voice was a little breathless.

He jumped, and stared, and his eyes widened incredulously as he walked towards her rather like a man who couldn't believe his senses.

"Cripes. What in the name of heaven are you doing here?" He sat heavily in a chair beside her and looked at her, taking in every detail of her appearance. "What made you choose this place for a holiday?"

"What made you?" she countered.

Pedro asked if Clive wanted dinner but he had eaten on the 'plane so he and Lynn walked through the café to the tables on the terrace and Clive chose a table that was more isolated than the others, on the far side of the outdoor space. He ordered coffees and while they were waiting they sat opposite each other without speaking. It was as if each was getting a second wind. Lynn certainly felt as if she were re-grouping and marshalling her thoughts. It was a natural assumption that she should be on holiday, she supposed, but thought he would soon think it strange she had come to such a one-eyed place alone. It was much more a honeymoon place. Was Clive hoping to make it that?

When the coffee came she helped herself to sugar and pushed the bowl to him. He unwrapped a packet, then screwed up the paper. "Where were we?" he asked and she guessed his mind was exploring all avenues in connection with her being here. Had he any clues to the right explanation?

She drew a deep breath. "This is hardly a holiday place."

"Spain is very attractive at this time of the year—sun, colour, warmth." He began unwrapping another piece of sugar. "Artists live here all the year round. I believe there is an artists' colony along the coast."

She decided to be honest. "I'm here because I'm on the Tracey case."

Once again his mouth dropped and then shut as his eyes narrowed.

"That's why I left Hendon's. Mrs. Tracey wasn't satisfied with your handling of it so she asked me to take it on."

Clive swore under his breath, not in the least amused. Lynn knew him well enough to know that he was put out and—what was unusual for him—really annoyed.

"The file was closed," she said defensively.

"Of all the silly interfering women . . ."

"I beg your pardon." Lynn's voice was hard.

"Well, aren't you?"

"No, I am not."

"That's a matter of opinion." He

unwrapped another knob of sugar. "How the heck did you get yourself here?"

"By plane," she snapped.

"Lay off. You know what I mean. There's no need to crack jokes. This isn't funny."

She hid a sudden smile. It wasn't, of course, but she couldn't help being amused because he was so put out. "Of course it isn't. I'm here on the job." She looked at him and met his eyes. They were cold and more grey than blue.

He was silent. Lynn watched the expressions playing over his face and waited. The next move was his.

"This is darned awkward."

Lynn raised her eyebrows. It wasn't for her.

"You've no idea what a pain in the neck you are." She laughed aloud, and shrugged.

"Oh, be quiet," he snapped, and Lynn had her first inkling that the situation was truly serious in his eyes.

She sat quietly but now she was more at one with him and had the feeling that they must stop sparring and discuss the Joan Tracey situation in a mature fashion.

"You've guessed I'm not here on a holiday," he said at last and Lynn found herself relaxing. He wasn't ready to be amiable but he was ready to be reasonable.

"Yes," she agreed quietly.

"I'm here on the Tracey case in a sense." He obviously wasn't ready to talk fully so Lynn drank her coffee and looked around. The outside café of the Miranda was sparsely patronised, there was a TV inside and most of the patrons were there, but it was lit with coloured lights strung round this space and across it, and had the effect of being a patch of colour in the night darkness, though the night wasn't dark if you looked into it. Lynn stared beyond the lights across the road, lined with palms, across the narrow strand with the white breaking waves and out to sea. She could see the lights of the fishermen's boats and rising darkly the land mass of the island. How far was it, she wondered, and guessed it must be farther than it looked. Distances at sea were deceptive.

"You've staggered me," Clive said at last.

Lynn turned and gave him all her attention.

"Well, I was surprised to see you," she admitted.

"No, I wasn't meaning that exactly. I meant in your taking the case."

"I was a bit surprised myself," Lynn admitted swallowing a chuckle. Clive looked too grave to be ready to be amused. It was unlike him. He was usually—well, almost flippant about work. It was one of his maxims that one could work as efficiently when one was gay as when one was dull.

"It's shaken me. If any one had asked me if you were likely to do the unexpected I'd have said NO in capital letters."

"Humph," grunted Lynn and felt her spirits rising. She wasn't in the office now and said so. "There I was a secretary. I wasn't me."

"But . . ." he gave a slight smile ". . . the me would have showed itself in most people."

Lynn hesitated. "It probably did but you were too—er—busy to see it."

His eyes met hers and she knew he knew that she was letting him down lightly. He was aware that she was calling him self-centred and selfish without using those words. He shifted his seat and fiddled for a moment with his tie.

With some sympathy Lynn changed the conversation. "Does Mrs. Tracey know you've re-opened the case?"

"It hasn't been re-opened. It was never closed in my mind." He spoke defensively and stared at her and Lynn saw that his eyes were more blue than grey now, and she felt her interest quickening as she sensed he was ready to discuss the position —to a point.

She said mildly. "The file was marked closed."

He grunted.

"I think if you had meant to go on, even on your own you could have given Mrs. Tracey some hope. She needs comfort."

He raised his eyes to heaven, but agreed that that had been a difficult aspect of the case.

"I don't see why."

"You wouldn't." He looked at his empty coffee cup and looked at her.

"I don't want any more, thanks."

He called the boy and ordered one for himself. Then he continued. "There are some odd aspects in this case."

"I couldn't agree more," she breathed.

"Oh?" He was alert. "What have you discovered?"

"That you didn't file all the knowledge you had on the Tracey file. You knew Joan Tracey was learning Spanish."

"Yes, but after I'd learned that and before I returned to London from North Faldon, I'd learned more."

It was on his return from the North that he had decided Hendon's were going to drop the Tracey case. Lynn waited.

"I wonder if you've any knowledge that I haven't?" He looked at her calculatingly. "Or any suspicions?"

"Possibly." She wasn't going to give anything away.

"Then supposing we team up about Joan Tracey and see where we stand?" When she hesitated he said quite seriously and not disparaging her ability. "I think it would be better if we did. We can probably each contribute something."

His manner again warned Lynn that he thought the case serious. She'd no means of telling yet how serious, but she thrilled to the idea of their working together on something that seemed as if it might be big. She never saw that there could be danger in it, or that he might be deliberately leading her on.

He told her why he advised Hendon's should give up the case. "It's more than just a missing person. In the beginning I believe Joan did leave home because she couldn't stand that artificial atmosphere any longer and felt she must get away on her own. There was obviously no intention of disappearing. She worked near enough home to go back whenever she wanted and to phone any time without it being too expensive—not that money seems to have mattered."

Lynn nodded following the re-cap carefully. There was nothing new yet.

"I think . . ." Clive was talking consideringly now ". . . that it was when she went to North Faldon that the idea of vanishing was born."

"She covered her tracks well."

"And gave no cause for suspicion at first. It was a gradual fading out. Her letters grew less and less."

"So?" Still no new ground, Lynn thought.

"It was arranged. Something happened

while she was working away from home at the hospital that set the idea in motion."

"The man she visited!"

"Yes."

"It isn't you then?" Lynn exclaimed.

Clive looked at her blankly.

"When you arrived here out-of-the-blue I thought you might be the man."

"Heaven preserve me," he gasped. "Talk about an imagination. I've never even seen the girl."

"But I didn't know that," Lynn protested. "It seemed feasible. It could have been the reason for your dropping the case."

"Any more bright ideas?"

She grinned. "Not at the moment. Let me hear yours."

"Mine are facts," he said with emphasis. "It's the man in Joan's life that I am anxious to learn about."

He told her part of what he had learned about the man with whom they both believed she had come to Spain.

"He was in the London hospital being patched up after a prison brawl. It wasn't easy to get the details but I tracked down a fellow who'd recently been released from prison and that's the story he told. It fits the facts. This fellow of Joan's—er, Charles Edgar—seems to have been a minor cog in a big-time drug ring. He got a light sentence because nothing much was proved against him and the dope ring wasn't broken."

Lynn licked her lips. This revelation was more than she had bargained for. It sounded as if Joan had got a bad egg.

"I believe the Boss of the gang has been lying doggo and that Charles Edgar will contact him and the whole filthy business will re-start."

Lynn listened to the story, digesting the facts. Clive had talked to reporters and "friends in the know" and Hendon's had their own grapevine.

"Do you think Joan knows all this?" Lynn asked.

"No-o, but she must know something or she wouldn't have agreed to run off here, would she?"

"I don't see why not. Her silence was probably because she had fallen in love with a man with a prison record. Can you imagine her telling Mr. and Mrs. Tracey and taking Charles Edgar home? She probably felt her only course was to disappear."

They sat and talked until past midnight, going backwards and forwards and viewing all the known facts but not getting anywhere different from Clive's contention that Charles Edgar would link up with the Boss in Flavidest.

That had come via the grapevine. But they'd no knowledge of the man known as the Boss. Without his saying so Lynn knew Clive was after him, to smash the drug business. She thought of Joan.

"If Charles Edgar loved her . . ." Her voice died. Charles Edgar might have no moral scruples to prevent his trafficking in drugs but that didn't mean he couldn't love Joan or that she couldn't love him.

They went on talking. "How did you discover Flavidest?" Lynn asked when she had told him all she had learned at North Faldon.

"By sheer hard work and a few lucky breaks," was the somewhat evasive reply. Clive having learned of the Spanish lessons, guessed Spain would be the couple's destination. By visiting all the travel agencies in North Faldon and adroit questioning, asking for suggestions on out-of-the-way places, he had learned of Flavidest and the fact that "Some local people have chosen it for a winter break."

Putting two and two together Lynn and Clive deduced that Joan had left North Faldon to hide her tracks and that Mrs. Wilson had collected the travel tickets and taken them to her. That was the reason for the visit about which Lynn had heard.

The picture was coming clear, but it was only of the past. It didn't give Lynn a clue how she ought to proceed.

Clive admitted, "There's more to it than I've told you, Lynn. Various bits of proof and complications."

Lynn looked at him steadily. "I suppose I've got to take them for granted—the proofs I mean. What about the complications?"

Clive's reply wasn't a direct answer to the question. "A reporter fellow told me the Boss had a cast iron alibi. That's how he slipped the police net. He also said nothing will keep him out of the drug racket for long. He likes the big money."

"Why don't the police nab him?"

"How the woman talks! I've no doubt they would if they knew him."

He looked at her again in his considering way and rather irritably Lynn snapped at him to tell her the rest. She thought as the Boss had an alibi he must be known.

"I mean whoever he is there wasn't a hint of suspicion against him," Clive explained.

"Tell me the rest," she said again. She knew he was keeping something back.

He shook his head. "You know all that is your business. You're not on the drug case. You're on Joan Tracey's. That's your job. I reckon the girl will need a shoulder when she learns what she's married."

"They are married then?"

Lynn thought he hesitated. "I saw the entry at the registrar's."

Lynn shivered. Poor Joan.

"Cold?" Clive asked and imperceptibly the atmosphere between them changed. They didn't forget the situation surrounding Joan Tracey but they did push it to the back of their minds. "We can't do anything about it tonight," Clive pointed out and declared that his brain wasn't clear. "Finding you here has got me addled. Shall we go for a stroll? Do you know a place called O'Connell's?"

Lynn shook her head.

"We'll visit it tomorrow," and that was all he would say. Flavidest was a small fishing village but it was by no means a dull one. It was well past midnight but all the cafés and snack dancing bars were open with music coming from them.

As they crossed the road and then walked towards the harbour, Lynn realised it wasn't as sheltered here as it had been at the Miranda and began putting her arms in her cardigan. As Clive waited she felt him looking at his brooch on her frock and she touched it lightly. "I've grown fond of it," she said naturally.

She couldn't see his face as they resumed their walking but his voice sounded pleased. "I thought it looked like you."

Lynn weighed the words and was surprised. She thought they sounded complimentary. It was the first compliment Clive had ever paid her.

When they came to a step in the pavement he took her arm, and they walked on with his hand round the bend of her elbow. "It's impossible to believe we've come from English frosts to Spanish sunshine," he said, and as she nodded she felt the amusement welling up in him. "Is there an illustration there?"

"Meaning?" she asked and was conscious of him as an attractive companion.

"In London I always thought you a bit frosty . . ."

She pushed his hand away, spluttering.

Laughing unaffectedly he put it back and held her arm firmly. "It's the truth. I never thought you liked me half as much as you liked Ellis."

"I didn't."

"Why not?"

"You never tried to be nice . . ."

"Did he? Did he hold your hand and make love to you? He's a married man . . ."

"Of course he didn't, but he did behave as if he liked me." Lynn laughed, conscious of her new found freedom and rejoicing. "I never felt I was only part of the fittings with him."

"Ah-h," Clive breathed. "I seem to have heard that sentiment before."

She frowned at him, searching her mind.

"After you gave in your notice you said I only saw you as part of the furniture. Didn't you?"

"Did I? It was true, so probably I did."

"Rubbish. You always made it quite clear that I was the feckless, junior partner, not worth a second thought." His grip on her arm tightened and she knew he was enjoying himself. "You cramped my style."

They walked along the broad arm of the harbour that Lynn could see from her bedroom and where the tide ran up in waves and occasionally burst in unexpected spray.

"English frosts," he murmured and when he felt her stiffen and draw away warningly he went on, "Spanish sunshine. I could thaw myself, be uninhibited, carefree, jump over the moon. I shall look forward to getting to know Miss Lynn Laurel in the Spanish sunshine."

6

NEXT day was another lovely day, with a blue sea and a blue sky. Lynn stood on her balcony before breakfast and watched the sky brighten as the sun cleared the mountains. Vaguely she wondered what weather they were having in London but found it hard to imagine frosts, hail, snow or even a bright sun accompanied by a cold north-easter as she stood in the warm early morning air. She looked at the balcony next door and thought it was Clive's bedroom. He was downstairs waiting for her in the lounge.

As there was a high wind blowing they had breakfast in the café-restaurant.

"It's a feature of the coast at this time of year Pedro was telling me," Clive said explaining why they were to eat indoors. "Everything outside is covered with a fine layer of sand."

As Lynn poured their coffee Pedro came up, beaming as always. "The wind." He shrugged. "As my friend from England last year says, the cobwebs, they go. And the wind it will go by midday."

Lynn listened smilingly and revelled in the sudden realisation that life was full and interesting and she was on her own—almost. Being truthful she admitted she was glad Clive was with her on the case. She didn't think she could have handled it alone with the developments he foresaw.

He was dressed in holiday attire, with light trousers and a zig-zag blue and yellow striped shirt, and he had a camera hanging over the back of his chair. The colours in his shirt picked up the colours in her frock.

"What a day," he said conventionally enough and later as they battled against the wind along the beach at the water's edge he explained. "We are tourists. We must act our part. Have you a camera?"

"No."

"Never mind, I've two."

She raised her eyebrows and was going to make some remark about pessimistically having two strings when he explained. "Stills and a ciné." He had the stills and took her with the wind blowing the dark hair across her face and the waves breaking in spray as the sand stung the backs of her legs. "It would have been better on ciné . . ." He talked technically and Lynn realised photography was one of his hobbies.

Heads down they walked and talked, disjointedly because of the buffeting weather. Lynn glanced at the short promenade and marvelled at the way the palms were bending in the wind.

"I suppose we take it for granted we team together, up to a point," he said. Lynn nodded. The idea that they might work separately—or that she might leave the Tracey case to him—had not entered her head.

He was walking with his hands clasped behind his back. She was clutching hers round her, with her handbag under her arm. "We'll be blown back," she shouted as the wind snatched her words.

He didn't hear. He put out his hand and drew her closer. "Our first job is to locate Joan Tracey and Charles Edgar, and then to persuade Joan to leave him."

They turned and walked up to the

promenade where it was sheltered, and prepared to walk back.

"Phew," Lynn relaxed and pushed the hair off her face then rubbed her eyes to clear them of sand and salt. She hadn't been able to wear sun-specs, the wind was too strong.

"Quite a battle," he grinned, "but it's helped to create the right picture. Going out into an inferno like that is typical of the English tourist. That's our rôle."

Lynn chuckled. Working in the office with Clive she had appreciated his thoroughness. Working on the job with him she saw it in action and was even more appreciative. He thought things through, though she was surprised that he was at pains to prevent their being suspect. It hadn't struck her that they might be in that category to anyone. Little tremors ran up her spine and she lifted her head as if to say, "Come on."

That was rather how she felt, ready for anything.

"I think I'd better tie up my hair."

While she fetched a scarf from the Miranda he collected his ciné camera and gave her the other.

"But I don't know anything about taking photos." His was obviously complicated. Cameras had to be foolproof for her.

"Don't worry, you won't have to. I'll take all we want. It's window dressing for you."

"As long as I'm not being made a porter . . ."

He ignored her but as they walked on, getting what shelter from the wind they could, he glanced at her and said, "Look as if you are enjoying yourself."

She was going to snap back, she had been puzzling over the job they were on when she realised she had been frowning.

"We are on holiday," he reminded her.

She laughed and thought what an extraordinary twist circumstances had taken that she should seem to be on holiday with Clive Hendon.

"Look as if you're enjoying yourself," he said again.

"I'll try," she said and found the job easy. She was enjoying herself. She was appreciating her new self and the possibilities she saw unfolding.

They went to the post office and bought

stamps, "For cards," Clive reminded her and asked how many she wanted.

"Two, that's all. One to Mother, one to Dad."

They bought their cards and found a sheltered seat along the far side of the harbour where they could sit in the sun and write them. Clive spoke good Spanish so the shopping had been easy. It would help in their getting about, Lynn realised.

He led the conversation. He sat opposite her and looked at her in that way that wasn't aggressive but was confidently masculine. "Do you know, I realise that I don't know much about you." He was referring to the fact that her mother and father were divorced.

She shrugged, hiding a smile as she replied, "Ellis knew the family set up."

He was unabashed. "I'm glad I didn't. Now I shall have the pleasure of getting to know you." He hummed the song, "Getting to know you," and nodded as if it was something he was determined to enjoy.

She was to learn as they worked together that although he might enjoy the circumstances in which they found themselves, he never lost sight of the reason for their being in Flavidest.

As they sat on in the sun after the cards were written he lifted his camera and held it to his eye as if he were considering views. "It's an excellent cover-up," he said. "I can stare at that house on the rock while I appear to be contemplating a photo of the church tower. Do you see?"

Lynn did, and she saw also how much pleasanter it was to work with Clive as a colleague than as a boss. While he walked round, using the cameras to examine the rock face up which the houses seemed to climb, Lynn jotted down some notes in shorthand. Chiefly it was for something to do. She didn't want to stare at Clive with open-mouthed admiration! There were no notes she felt ought to be made for the case, so she wrote her impressions of the Miranda. She often found once she had written a thing she had a clearer picture in her mind. That's how she had often got a hunch at Hendon's when she transcribed back.

She wrote that the Miranda was a small hotel, staffed almost exclusively by the family. It was a popular local rendezvous and seemed to be open all the hours there were. It had been open when she and Clive returned after midnight from their walk. Men had been having breakfast when she woke this morning and long before the light had come over the hills. Possibly Flavidest was on the route to some big centre and the Miranda acted as transport café.

"What's that doodling?" Clive asked. He had joined her while she was intent on the shorthand.

"Nothing private," she said airily and held it out to him.

He shook his head. "Double Dutch as far as I'm concerned."

"I should have thought you'd have found a knowledge of shorthand useful."

"I don't like notes on paper when I'm on a job. It's safer to keep them in your head."

Anyone would think his usual work was on the lines of MI5 Lynn thought with a slight spurt of irritation. There was no doubt Clive Hendon fancied himself. In his own eyes he was the cat's whiskers. Quickly she scribbled over the notes she'd made and flipping over the pages began

106

writing in longhand the names of the flowers she had recognised. "Marigolds or something very similar. Rock roses. Grape hyacinths. Red hot pokers."

As she wrote she was aware that Clive had drifted away again and she was amazed at herself for the spurt of annoyance. Why should she feel annoyed? She could make notes if she liked. He wasn't her boss.

Of course he wasn't. The knowledge hit Lynn with fresh impact and she viewed her new freedom with an uplifting heart so that she was smiling when he came back with a local guide book.

He blinked and nodded to himself.

"What have you discovered?" she asked.

"That my knowledge of human nature is increasing."

"Cocky."

"It's a fact. I can understand why people dash to sunnier climes in February and March. Look at us. If we were in Hendon's . . ."

"Heaven forbid," Lynn ejaculated.

"Did you hate it then?"

"Not at the time, but I would if I had to go back."

He looked stunned, and then grinned with mock humility. "Perhaps I don't know human nature as well as I thought." He waited but Lynn was silent, so he looked at the map.

"From Hendon's grapevine I learned we must visit O'Connell's Bar. Here's the map. Apparently it's one of *the* tourist attractions."

"It sounds Irish."

"What perspicuity. You could be right."

Lynn threw a dead marigold at him.

They walked round the small shopping centre, then strolled among the parked cars on the avenue behind the front and in the square. The two English cars came in for some unobtrusive scrutiny and any English voice in the shops was arresting, but they saw and learned nothing that might be a clue to Joan Tracey's whereabouts.

"Oughtn't we to do something more definite?" Lynn asked and suggested, "go to the information office?"

"No. Not yet at any rate. When we do call in authority it will be the police."

"We seem to be muddling about."

"It's my way of doing the job." His mouth was firm then he began to laugh. "Don't tell me, I know what you're going to say. It's not yours, and I'm not your boss."

Lynn blinked and bit her lip. She had. To her mind they were going round the case instead of getting down to it. Clive seemed content to behave as if they really were on holiday. A brief suspicion swept Lynn and she wondered if he could be kidding her, that he was the man in Joan Tracey's life but she swept it aside as he asked a question.

"Will that suit madam?"

"What? I wasn't listening."

"We work my way today and yours tomorrow?"

"And you will work on the basis that it is always today and never tomorrow, I bet," she said crisply.

"How well you know me," he agreed blandly, and turned her towards a wide alley that was a series of steps and led to the short high promontory above the harbour. "I think it's time we tried to find our first clue." Near the top on the right hand side there was an open door. It was O'Connell's bar.

"Sangria. That's the special drink," Clive told her and ordered two when they were inside. It was a dark cluttered place, with low seats and low tables and overlapping mats and rugs, on the floor.

Dan O'Connell served them. He still spoke with an Irish accent and had a real welcome for the travellers, as he termed them, and asked where they came from. He nodded when Clive said England and though he asked no questions he was ready enough to answer any that Clive asked.

It was a slack time for tourists though they didn't have multitudes in Flavidest at any time, "Just the nice number to make the place pleasant if you see what I mean, without they take over the entoire joint."

"I suppose this is one of the show places?" Clive looked round.

"Sure, sure. 'Tis known the world over. There's not a soul that comes to Flavidest and stays the night but doesn't come to O'Connell's. You'll find it in the guide now." He showed Clive and was led to talk of recent visitors.

"Have you seen an English couple lately?" Clive asked. "They could be friends of ours. We heard they might be coming this way."

"Did you now?" Dan frowned thoughtfully, they may have he seemed to say but said aloud, "The English are mostly honeymooners at this time of the year. And a bumper time it is too, for the artists' colony. Most of them like to buy the landscape."

Clive was nodding while Lynn digested the information when Dan asked with a sly wink, "You two wouldn't be on your honeymoon now, would you?"

Lynn choked. Clive ordered refills.

Dan didn't wait for an answer but mixed the drinks and then stood in the doorway and talked to his dog.

Lynn looked at Clive but he was sitting back and in the dim light she couldn't see his eyes to read their expression.

"Good morning, how are you?" A smiling face came round Dan O'Connell and Lynn recognised her taxi driver.

"Hello, Guan," she greeted him.

He attached himself to them as guide. "No coach today. You are lucky. I am free."

As they left Dan told them to come again. He turned up his radio and grinned at their surprise on hearing London. "If you want any London news you know where to come," he said.

Guan made them continue up the alley to the plateau that looked over the harbour and round beyond the cove to the vast sweep of the bay. He talked in French but when he heard Clive speak in Spanish he thankfully lapsed into his own tongue. He told them Dan O'Connell had been in Flavidest ten years "and the tourists all like him."

He took them to the church, to the remains of the castle and showed them the monument to a local boy who had made good.

Then, beaming as if they were the *pieces de resistance*, he took them to the telescopes. The end of the plateau was set out as a park, with seats, flower beds, a dovecote and the three telescopes, one facing south, one east and one west.

Actually each could swivel so that it

overlapped the others but Clive chose the one facing south and trained it on the island. Then he put in the pesetas and he and Lynn each had a turn. As far as either could see it was uninhabited, there was no movement and no animals although there was a tumbledown building above the only bay on this side.

"What is it?" Clive asked.

He translated as Guan told him. It was a tourist attraction in the summer when the boats took parties for picnics on the island. Once some families had lived there but it was uninhabited now.

Both Lynn and Clive had the same thought. It would make a good hideout for a man who was waiting for a rendezvous and had no wish to be seen. The looks they exchanged as their time ran out on the telescope were enough.

They'd no chance to talk. Guan piloted them along the harbour arm they'd walked down last night. Pedro was right. It was midday and the wind had dropped to near dead calm. The leaves of the trees rustled faintly but the sea was waveless throwing back facets of light as the sun played on it. Lynn put on her sun specs and sat

113

beside Clive on a pile of planks. Casually he put his camera to his eye and appeared to be considering the promontory they'd left as a desirable subject.

Lynn looked at the pavement cafés, sparsely populated as far as she could see by the locals. There were certainly no outstandingly looking English among them. Had O'Connell seen Joan Tracey and Charles Edgar? Instinctively Lynn felt he had, or knew something about them.

"Si . . ." Guan was tapping Clive's arm and in a moment Lynn found herself being photographed with the guide.

They lunched on the terrace sitting at a table where Lynn found she could see into the café. She saw the pink shirted man and wondered if he were a permanent idler. He was sitting in the same seat, lolling back with a peaked cap forward over his eyes.

Neither Lynn nor Clive mentioned their thoughts of the morning. The tables round were full. A party of two car loads, had taken the tables nearby and there was a hubbub of noise but still Lynn knew Clive didn't want to talk "business".

He asked if she'd thought of bathing. "I brought a swim suit with me," she admitted, "but I can't imagine it would be warm enough yet."

"I saw a fellow at seven o'clock this morning getting buffeted about . . ."

Their talk was pleasant, but formal, Lynn thought and soon realised why. It wasn't spontaneous. Each was putting on an act. But it wasn't a barrier between them, there was no disharmony because neither was quite natural.

As she sat back to wait for the final course Lynn glanced toward the café and again saw the pink shirted man. Instinctively her hand went to her brooch. She was wearing a flower patterned frock today, but she had pinned it in her favourite place for an ornament, on the shoulder.

Clive saw the move and his eyes went to the brooch and although his expression hardly changed she knew he was pleased.

She smiled inside. He was cocky that his present had pleased her so much.

They lunched and after a short siesta set off along the coast road and path over the cliffs for the artists' colony. "We might learn something. I'm not sure if O'Connell was trying to tell us Joan and Charles

Edgar were here or not," Clive said, "but we can talk with no one to hear—and it won't be wholly unenjoyable. At least, it won't from my point of view. So it fulfils one of the conditions I demand in my work, that I shall find it enjoyable."

Lynn smiled and let him talk. In some ways he had been withdrawn this morning. There had been understanding between them but he hadn't been his gay, flippant self. Now it seemed to be emerging.

When she mentioned it he asserted. "It's petticoat government, I can't adjust myself to it."

Lynn sighed exaggeratedly. "When have I been allowed to have a say in what we're going to do?"

He was unabashed. "Subconsciously you influence me all the time. Because you are with me I have to ask, can I do this, can I do that?"

"In other words I'm a drag?"

"A very attractive one," he said unexpectedly.

It was a pleasant cliff walk to the artists' colony and Lynn enjoyed sparring with Clive. It was the sort of thing that would be quite foreign to Jack Delmore, she thought, and wondered if she'd send him a card. She didn't know his address in Norway but she could send it to his London hotel. When she got home she'd arrange with her father for her visit to Edinburgh to meet Jack's people.

"Where have you gone to?" demanded an irritated voice. "This is the way you used to behave in the office—as if I wasn't about. Good heavens, girl, it's time someone taught you how to behave . . ."

"Supposing I came up with a thought that lit up the Tracey case?" she cut him short.

"That would be different." Some of the bantering left his manner. "What's the great idea?"

"I haven't one. I was just asking."

"Spare me," he breathed. "Here I am yoked in partnership with . . ." He looked at her. She returned his look. And then they discussed the island as a probable refuge for Joan and Charles Edgar while he waited for the Boss.

"If they are there someone must have taken them across. We might hear of such a trip."

"Unless they stole a boat and took themselves," Lynn suggested.

"Then there'd be a hue and cry for the boat and we'd have heard of that from Guan. And if they'd bought a boat it would be gossip."

Arguing amicably and not too seriously they walked on, but Clive was serious when he declared, "Dan O'Connell is in on this. He knows something. We'll have to walk warily. We aren't in on it. We're tourists. When he mentioned the wireless and London news that could have meant quite a lot."

The path dropped down through the trees and the giant cactus to the settlement and in a few minutes they were at the bay where artists of different nationalities had gathered.

They wandered round, peering into open doorways, strolling round small galleries.

But they failed to pick up any clues. By adroit questioning Clive learned that the artists had had no visitors for the past three weeks.

They were strolling up the main street,

when a motor horn thrust itself upon them and there was Guan in his taxi.

"I saw you," he said blandly and opened the door for Lynn to go in the back while he indicated that Clive should sit beside him.

He took them to the quayside at Flavidest where the fishing fleet was coming in and stood with them while they watched the boats unload their catches into smaller boats or bring it alongside and pass it over in boxes and baskets, to be carried to the stone building that was the fish auction.

It was a smelly, gruesome business, Lynn thought and hated it. She looked in a shrinking fashion at the small octopuses that were so sought after and marvelled that they should be so tasty when served by Pedro. She'd had some last night. She didn't think she'd want any tonight!

Later she and Clive shared the same thought. Surely Guan wasn't keeping a watch on them?

7

AS Lynn changed for dinner her thoughts were pleasantly amusing. She chose a tangerine coloured frock that always gave an added glow to her skin. Now that she had caught the sun it seemed to give even more, and she laughed softly at herself, chidingly. Would she have dressed with such care if Clive had not been her companion?

Lynn was honest. Probably not—unless there had been another attractive young man staying at the Miranda. Clive was attractive. She was ready to admit that, admitting also that she had never really known him in the office. She had always judged him from a critical attitude, aware that she was only the-girl-in-the-office. How thankful she was she had stepped out of that dead end. Her eyes laughed back at her in the mirror, golden green because she was finding life exhilarating.

But it hadn't been a progressive day in connection with Joan Tracey. Lynn thought it must be written off as a blank. True she and Clive had explored several avenues and she had become convinced in her own mind that the most likely place Joan and Charles Edgar would have taken refuge was the island. If she'd been alone she'd have chartered a boat to take her across, but she had let herself be swayed by Clive. He was handling the case whatever he said about their being partners.

Lynn breathed deeply. The air was warm and sweetly scented. She didn't recognise the scent but it was subtle—and as she stared out over the dark night sea, she felt disinclined to focus her attention on the job she'd come to do. She felt happy to dream, to wonder. Tomorrow she would get down to it, really tackle the job and refuse to be side-tracked by Clive. For the moment . . .

With her eyes on the island she wondered about Joan and Charles Edgar. Clive said they were married. Was he a fortune hunter? Was he a man who was likely to fall foul of the law again? Was Clive right that this Charles was in a big drug racket? Her heart went out to Joan.

On such an evening Lynn found it hard

to concentrate on the problem, but she was instinctively sure Clive knew more than he'd shared.

With a sudden awareness that she had been dreaming too long she looked at her watch and hurried. Dinner was always a late meal, but tonight she made it later than usual.

"You have decided to eat then?" Clive asked getting up lazily from one of the deepest chairs in the lounge.

"I'm sorry, I forgot the time."

"As long as you didn't forget me," he murmured.

She raised her eyebrows and sensed that his mood was like hers. They had both succumbed to the charm of Flavidest and wanted nothing but to enjoy it. Tomorrow would do for work.

She appreciated his light suit with the pale shirt and darker tie and thought how much more attractive he looked here than he had done at Hendon's.

"Hendon's needs painting," she said.

He blinked and brought his mind to take in her words by an effort. "What made you say that at this particular moment in time?"

122

She didn't explain that she thought Hendon's could be made to frame him more effectively if it were gayer and brighter. She was too surprised at the thought herself.

"You'd probably find it easier to get a secretary if you cheered the place up."

"So you know we haven't got one?"

"Irene told me in her letter."

"So you are corresponding?"

"Ellis asked me to let him know how I get on. So I wrote to Irene."

To Lynn's surprise Clive's face flushed and he changed the conversation by picking up the menu and commenting on the varied assortment of food for every course.

Lynn smiled to herself. What had upset his lordship? Was he conscious that Ellis had been more considerate than he had?

If he were, he didn't let it spoil their evening. After dinner they strolled along to the harbour and went to a café where there was music and dancing.

"I wonder what they'd say at home if they could see us now?" Clive lived with Ellis and Irene. He leaned forward. "I wonder what they'd think?"

"How fortunate we are to be having such lovely weather," she replied demurely.

He grinned. "I think we are, too. Moonlight and roses in March . . . and a companion with whom to share them."

She smiled but felt a stop in her mind. Clive was charming, he was treating her as any woman would like to be treated on such a night but . . . He wasn't quite natural.

He wasn't really at ease. The phrases weren't slipping off his tongue with their usual facility. Possibly he found it hard to sustain the light flippant rôle for any length of time? Perhaps she wasn't the right audience? He probably remembered their relationship in the office and thought she knew him too well. It was funny they'd never really liked each other in the office. He was a nice fellow and a good companion.

She wondered. Supposing she had met him out here for the first time? What would be her reactions? She'd think he was attractive, she'd think he was fun, she'd think he was a good timer.

And she'd be right.

Lynn laughed at him across the small table and let her mood of inconsequence meet his. It was a night to be enjoyed. Not a night to be serious and introspective and ask "if" and say "but". He responded. They danced, they laughed, they teased one another and they walked home with their arms entwined and lingered over a goodnight kiss. But it wasn't too meaningful, simply in tune with the night and the soft sweet scent that filled the air.

Next morning it was obvious that they were both in a different mood. Lynn woke feeling vaguely uneasy and then she remembered. Last night.

She went to breakfast in a quiet frame of mind and her eyes searched his face. What she saw reassured her. He seemed to be searching her face and to be relieved at what he saw. His expression lightened and they went outside for breakfast talking about the contrast of this morning's calm with yesterday's wind.

"We'll have to make plans," he said.

She nodded and poured the coffee.

They made plans after breakfast, away from the Miranda, sitting out on the harbour arm. The sea was running up the outside of the wall but had no power today to break over them in spray. It was a deep blue and dead calm.

Lynn looked at the colourful boats in the harbour and lying on the beach, and then turned slightly towards Clive as he began to speak. "We've got the time factor to consider."

She raised her eyebrows. She didn't think he'd shown much consideration for it yesterday, and said so with some asperity. She wasn't feeling in tune with Clive today. Was there something aggressive in his attitude?

"We made contact with O'Connell. We couldn't do more," he said. "I'm waiting for information from London."

Lynn stared at him and felt her irritation rising. It struck her that he had let her waste a whole day in her search for Joan, and she said so.

"Of course I didn't. What would you have done differently?"

She shrugged, unable to answer, but she felt she had let him have his way when she ought to have acted on her own initiative. She was being paid by Mrs. Tracey and had no right to let herself get side tracked into dalliance however pleasant. She ought to have talked to Dan O'Connell. She said so. "I think I will."

"Heaven forbid! You'll do nothing of the sort."

Lynn's eyebrows went up. "What did you say?"

"That you will not let O'Connell know we have any interest in Joan Tracey or Charles Edgar."

"But he as good as said if we wanted news . . ."

"Cripes. Preserve me. I'll use him when I'm ready. Haven't you got it yet? This is NOT—repeat NOT—just a case of a missing girl. I'm here to learn the identity of the Boss and smash a drug ring. That's our first priority."

"Ours?"

"Yes ours." His eyes, more grey than blue, stared into hers. "Let's get this straight, Lynn. You're an amateur at this job. I'll help you out. We'll find Joan. But my part of the job is the more important, and must have priority."

Lynn swallowed. The damn masculine superiority.

He was continuing, a slight frown

between his eyes as he concentrated on what he was saying, as if he were dictating a report for the file at Hendon's.

In spite of herself Lynn respected the way he was handling the job step by step.

"I'm going to find Charles Edgar. That shouldn't be too difficult now we've contacted O'Connell. He's a wily one. He knows our visit wasn't casual but we'll string him along." Clive grinned with sudden, almost impish pleasure. "We'll find Charles Edgar and Charles shall lead me to the Boss. In the meantime . . . But just a sec," he interrupted himself and whipping out his camera he took Lynn's photo after some play at studying light and background to get the perfect picture. "We musn't look too serious. This is what I propose . . ."

Lynn found herself listening hypnotised.

He was going to hire a car and drive to Malafedia. "That's a town about eighty kilometres inland to the South West. I don't know anything about it but we may be able to get a guide book that will tell us something, though I don't suppose it's much of a tourist resort."

"Why Malafedia?" Lynn asked, trying to adjust her thoughts. Her inclination was to tell him to scram, but she wasn't as silly as to follow her personal feelings. She was on a job and meant to bring it to a satisfactory conclusion. She realised she'd need some help, she knew he was the person to give it; she was also beginning to feel involved in his side of affairs.

"I want to make a phone call to London."

"And there are no phones in Flavidest?" She enquired sarcastically.

"It's not that. But strangers are noticeable in small places in slack seasons and to hire a car and explore the country is in true tourist tradition."

"I hope you'll remember to drive on the right," she said, half-sulkily.

She was puzzled. For whom was Clive working? He was going to tie up the Joan Tracey case as part of the Charles Edgar file. It would be a philanthropic gesture to Mrs. Tracey, but surely he wasn't working from such motives on the Charles Edgar business? Ellis was in it. It was on Hendon's books. Who was sponsoring the investigation?

Guan was at the garage. "I drive you, wherever you want to go," he smiled.

Clive shook his head. He wanted to hire a car to drive himself—and Lynn. He playfully punched Guan in the ribs and Lynn felt herself blushing as Guan laughed with joyous understanding and waved them on their way with nods and sly glances.

"That's satisfied him," said Clive, well-pleased.

He phoned London at Malafedia, getting through without delay. He left Lynn in the car in a park near the centre of the small busy town. Malafedia was a packing and distributing place for the oranges and lemons grown in the district and also had cellars that produced a light red wine from the locally grown grapes.

As she sat in the car, in the shade of some acacias and very tall palms Lynn thought over the situation. Hendon's were dealing with the case from London. Clive hadn't told her any more.

If that was the way he felt about it . . . She shrugged but inside she was resentful, and that feeling stayed with her for the rest of the day.

They looked round the town for which Clive managed to buy a slim guide and saw the old church with the medieval houses clustering round, visited the cellars and tasted the wine and had lunch at a restaurant famous for its pastas and black coffee served after every meal.

Clive was in good form, pleased with himself and all the world. He told her he'd spoken to Ellis—but not what he'd learned. He enjoyed lunch, found the town to his liking and talked easily of nothing very much.

Lynn answered in monosyllables or nodded or shook her head. She felt let down. She told herself she was being unreasonable. Nevertheless she felt Clive had not played fair. He was cheerful and confident and was his masculinely arrogant self as he tried to make conversation.

He asked her about her home life and listened with every appearance of interest to her curt answers. When she made it too obvious that she was answering against her will he told her about his boyhood and some of his adventures in solving cases for Hendon's.

"It's a fine job. Men and women are so interesting."

Lynn nodded. They were.

When they returned the car Guan was waiting, "You have had the good day," he beamed.

"Very good," Clive nodded over-emphatically. "Haven't we, Lynn."

She glared at him. "The country was looking lovely. It must be wonderful in January when the almonds are in bloom."

In silence they walked to the Miranda. "What about a cup of tea?" he asked. It was nearly four-thirty and the Miranda made a good pot of tea.

She was going to refuse when he said sharply, "For heaven's sake stop sulking and grow up. We're on a job. This isn't a social outing."

She jumped and wanted to snap back but found herself speechless. Then she said slowly, as if it were a revelation, "Yes, we're on a job. I'll be down to dinner."

She asked Pedro to send tea to her bedroom and flopped on the bed.

The tea came with lemon instead of milk and Lynn was going to send it back in a spurt of irritation when she took a pull on herself.

She was behaving childishly. She might have justification for feeling that Clive had treated her badly but there was nothing she could do but accept it. Until she had some news of Joan Tracey to give Mrs. Tracey she was bound to Flavidest and Clive's company.

She might as well adjust herself to his odd behaviour. She didn't admire it. It didn't make her like him. But it didn't make him a poor agent for Hendon's. She admitted he was good at his job and nothing she had seen since they'd been here had given her any reason to alter that opinion. She saw now that he was giving his own case priority but that he did mean to help her.

She drank her tea thinking over the situation and her emotional involvement. That was wherein lay the trouble, in her emotions. She was hurt because she wasn't important to him. That wasn't fair, because he wasn't important to her.

From four until eight Lynn argued with herself, and at eight she got off the bed and began to dress for dinner. She had come to terms with herself. This was an episode. It wasn't an emotional interlude. It was a job of work that was so complicated that it was beyond her to complete, so she would be grateful for any help that came her way. She tossed up her head. She would accept Clive on his own terms.

At eight-thirty she went down to dinner. It was a pleasantly "civilised meal," that they sat over and then pushed back their chairs and sat over their coffee outside until it was late enough for Lynn to declare she felt like an early night.

Next morning she wakened refreshed and a little disappointed that she had let her emotions get so ruffled by anyone like Clive. She wore an off-white frock that made her look cool and feel cool, with green sandals and a green necklace.

Lynn felt him look at her closely and she returned his gaze with natural friendliness, remarking on the day. It was windless again and was obviously going to be warm. "It must be scorching here in the Summer."

He nodded.

"I wondered . . ." he began.

Lynn was attentive.

". . . if we might have a picnic lunch today?" He lowered his voice. "It's in keeping with our rôle of holiday-makers."

Lynn agreed, so Clive asked Pedro if it could be arranged although they hadn't ordered it last night.

It was no trouble at all, Pedro assured them but they would have to wait the short time. They understood?

Clive went to collect the car while Lynn waited for the lunch. She was sitting back with her eyes closed in the lounge, complimenting herself on her natural but slightly casual behaviour when a voice disturbed her.

"Signorina . . ."

She was immediately alert. It was the man in the pink shirt. She looked at him enquiringly.

With a slight bow he handed her the packed lunches.

"Oh—thank you." Was he part of the Miranda menage?

Clive arrived and she joined him with the question still in her mind. She wondered whether to mention it, and would have liked to do so because in some way the man's presence made her uneasy, but she shrank from his probable reaction. She'd no doubt he'd tell her she was letting her imagination run away with her and she must stick to facts when she was on a job. Hunches and flashes of insight were all right in an office where they could be examined away from the situation.

They took the road to Alicante. "I landed there," Lynn remarked. "I expect you did."

"Yes." They talked of the alternative, Valencia. "It's a place I'd like to see." He flashed her a look. "It sounds romantic."

"Not to me. It sounds nutty. Oh, no, that's Barcelona."

Lynn looked at the landscape, remembering it from the ride on her arrival and thought again that it was cowboy country with the outcrops of rock, patches of scrub and few trees.

She hadn't seen Alicante except the airport and found the parade under the palms with its mosaic wavy paving fascinating. Clive took photographs and they went shopping in a main street running up from the front. "If you want to buy anything this is the place," he told her. While she sat at a café eating an ice, he phoned London. Once again the connection was accomplished quickly and he was back with her in less than half an hour.

He ordered coffee and sat back smoking a cigar.

Lynn raised her eyebrows and hid a smile. He didn't look right. He looked like a little boy playing at being grown-up. "Do you like cigars?" she asked.

"Not much," he admitted.

She was about to ask why he was smoking one when she remembered it was part of his tourist rôle. She wasn't unfriendly but she wasn't friendly. When he offered to buy her a handbag while he was buying one for Irene she reminded him that Ellis and Irene had given her one recently.

"Something else then?" he asked.

She shook her head, smiling and polite. "No, thank you very much, but I'll look at these. I'd like to buy my mother something."

They had a picnic lunch. Clive had brought wine and two glasses and they ate in a small sandy cove where they found a large flat rock to sit on.

He raised his glass. "To us."

She nodded, "To our jobs," and bent her head quickly so that she need not see his expression. "Let's see what Pedro has given us."

She unpacked the hard-boiled eggs, packets of mixed meats, rolls, cheese and fruit.

"We shan't starve."

They were silent as they began the meal and Lynn was conscious that she might have been too stiff but she found it hard to behave as she wanted. She wanted to be natural and normal with him, and treat him as nobody in particular. He wasn't anybody in particular . . . She thought of Jack and wondered where he was and how soon she would see him after she got home. "How long do you think we shall be in Flavidest?" she broke the silence.

"You sound as if you want to get away."

"I want to get the job finished."

"Of course." His face became serious. "I've been thinking over the last phone call and sorting out what Ellis had to tell me. I've been thinking some more about Joan Tracey, and I reckon you ought to be in the picture a bit more."

Lynn stiffened a little in preparation and

waited quietly. Suddenly she felt natural and looked at him as she waited.

"Joan has got hold of a really bad egg."

"So I guessed."

"He's pretty deep in the drug racket, far deeper than anyone suspected."

Lynn asked some questions. Hendon's had contacts with reporters, the police and the grapevine.

Clive refilled her glass and ate some cheese. "Charles Edgar must be a plausible sort . . ."

Lynn interrupted abruptly, "Who are you working for?"

He jumped and hesitated. "His wife."

Lynn's eyes widened. Poor Joan, she thought once again.

"Partly that is. She doesn't want him back. She wants a divorce."

"Would it matter," Lynn asked and there was a hint of sarcasm in her voice, "if you told me how all that we know and guess is linked? You must know you can trust me . . ."

"Of course" He spoke hastily, then admitted, "I ought to have told you right away what we suspected and Ellis was confirming, but seeing you so unexpectedly put me off balance."

Lynn's surprise showed.

He grinned ruefully. "It's a fact. I don't know that I'm on it now." Then he continued in a business-like, matter of fact voice.

Hendon's had been called in by Mrs. Dawson to trace her husband who disappeared five years ago.

Lynn remembered the case vaguely, Mrs. Dawson wanted to marry again. Now she came to think about it, Lynn didn't remember seeing that file during her last two weeks.

Clive continued. Suddenly the two cases met. The Charles Edgar in the Tracey business was Charles Dawson, the missing husband.

Naturally they had checked. It wasn't guesswork. Ellis had come up with the final corroboration on the phone today. As Charles Edgar Clive had learned that their man had been in the London hospital after a brawl in prison in which he had been knocked about. "Apparently he always had a scar on the bridge of his nose and across his forehead. Now he's got a damaged knee as well."

"I think you might have told me this sooner."

"We-ell, apart from the shock of seeing you I wasn't absolutely sure of the facts as I said. I am now. There was just a chance that the man with Joan might not have been our Charles Edgar—Charles Dawson, I mean. There was a funny business about his release from prison. It was earlier than the scheduled date for Charles Edgar. But I'm afraid it's him all right. Ellis's checking has proved it."

Lynn ate without noticing very much what she was eating.

"They went through a form of marriage." Clive threw out the information.

"Yes, you said yesterday they were married." Lynn looked at him steadily and her heart went out to Joan as it had so often before and she began wondering how best she could help her and she knew she was glad Clive was on the job with her though she didn't feel friendly towards him. "What . . ." She couldn't bring herself to ask "what do we do next?" so she said, "What happens next?"

"The ball is in their court."

"Oh." Lynn knew that meant the Boss and his men or Charles Edgar. For her and Clive it must be a waiting game.

"Though it may not be so long. Ellis had a rumour that the Boss may be on his way. It may only be a rumour, a deliberate one, but it may be fact."

As usual they had dinner on the terrace but they had a new waiter—the man in the pink shirt. He wasn't wearing the pink shirt but Lynn had no doubt of his identity.

So he *was* employed at the Miranda, she thought, and dismissed him as she listened to Clive talking about the trip they'd made and the films and ciné he'd taken. She fingered her brooch because she was conscious of their new waiter. He wasn't a good one. He served clumsily and he muddled two orders.

"What's up with the fellow?" Clive asked. The service was usually impeccable. That had been one of the noticeable things about the Miranda. It might be a family hotel, but it was in the first-class category for service and cuisine. Lynn knew she couldn't tell him here that she felt uneasy about the man. It seemed obvious to her he wasn't a waiter. So what was he? She decided she'd talk it over with Clive when they went for their after dinner stroll but she wasn't given the opportunity.

A taxi drew up and a man got out. Lynn had her back to him but she saw Clive stiffen and grow alert.

"Oh ho," he breathed under his breath and gave all his attention to his food. "It looks as if we may not have to wait so long . . . no, don't look round."

But Lynn had done so, and her mouth sagged.

The man was Jack Delmore.

8

FOR a moment, of course, Lynn didn't believe her eyes. The man was like Jack Delmore. She blinked and stared again and then heard his voice as he paid the taxi and turned.

It was Jack Delmore.

She heard Clive muttering under his breath at her behaviour. What had he nattered? Something about not having to wait so long and then he had hissed at her not to look round.

She had done so, and here was Jack. She got to her feet and waited for his eyes to turn and meet hers.

"What the dickens do you think you're doing?" Clive demanded in a tight voice as he half rose and then sat down again.

For perhaps half a second Lynn's thoughts wavered and she thought that perhaps this might not be the Jack Delmore she knew but the Boss of the drug ring that Clive was expecting. Jack could have deceived her . . .

144

She laughed at herself. She was getting melodramatic.

"Jack!" Her voice rang out. He swung round and his eyes lit up.

"What the dickens. . . ?" Clive began again but his voice died.

Lynn was laughing and going to the steps to meet Jack. She was aware that Clive was sitting slackly watching. He had been mad with her and now he was discomforted.

"I can't believe this," Lynn laughed at Jack.

"It doesn't surprise me," he replied with a warm grin and his eyes ranged over her approvingly. "In fact, it would have surprised me if you hadn't been here. Though I must confess I hadn't expected so immediate a welcome. Where were you?" He looked at the terrace. "That's rather nice."

"I shan't be a sec," Lynn called over her shoulder to Clive and walked into the Reception with Jack. An agent in Paris had fixed the trip and Pedro had a room ready.

"It's a knockout," Lynn told him and her pleasure was apparent. "Come down

145

as soon as you're ready. I'll be finishing my dinner."

With a light step she walked back to Clive.

"That's Jack Delmore," she said happily and without any distaste ate up the cold cauliflower au gratin that was congealing on the plate.

Clive raised his eyebrows murmuring, "Cripes." They were still raised, Lynn noticed, when Jack joined them. He'd had a snack on the plane so he was ready for a meal. Pedro laid up for him beside Lynn.

"There is room for the place?" He smoothed the cloth. "That is very nice for everyone."

He served Jack himself and brought coffee for Lynn and Clive. Lynn then remembered to introduce the two men.

"I'd forgotten you don't know each other." She said their names. Jack looked up from his soup and nodded with a "nice to meet you" sort of mutter.

Clive looked at him steadily, repeating the name, "Jack Delmore."

Pigeon-holing him, Lynn thought with a little spurt of anger but it died as she turned to Jack again. After all, that sort of behaviour was part of Clive's life. He was on a job. She sensed that Clive didn't like Jack, but was ready to admit that was natural after his mistake in his identity.

A wide smile lit her face as she thought of it, but she was sympathetic too. Then she dismissed Jack's arrival and concentrated on his being here.

"Good food," he said and approved of the wine. "Sure you won't have wine instead of coffee?" Lynn shook her head. "What about you, Clive?" Jack had accepted Clive naturally; he told Lynn later he thought Clive must be staying at the Miranda, as a guest, and that the management had naturally seated them together.

Clive refused politely. He wasn't his usual assertive self but Lynn knew him well enough to know that he was recovering, and hid a smile. It was rather fun that Clive had been shaken. She thought she liked him better for having witnessed it. She'd always remember she had seen his Achilles heel.

Jack didn't bolt his meal but he didn't linger over it, and when he'd finished pushed back from the table and asked

Lynn if she minded if he smoked. He asked Clive to have a cigarette then said. "This is cigar land. I'd like to take a few back for the old man. What do you recommend?"

Clive told him those he'd had recommended and asked where he'd come from. It was a civilised conversation without any undercurrents on Jack's side but Lynn was conscious of restraint from Clive although he was putting on a good act.

He asked questions and made appropriate comments. Lynn wanted to laugh aloud but she contented herself with an inward chuckle.

Gradually Clive got the picture and looked at Lynn, almost with surprise, she thought.

Jack was on the Continent with his parents. "They're here to see all the sights you Britishers take in your annual holidays, and I'm with them. We got to Paris . . ."

Lynn leaned forward remembering her one week in Paris with mother when she was fifteen and expecting him to talk about it, but he was saying:

"I had to phone Lynn's Pop while I was there . . ." He looked at her. "That machinery in Norway could do one of our jobs in half the time. I phoned your Pop and when he told me you were in Spain, Lynn, I reckoned it was an opportunity to flip down and see you."

"He gave you my address." Lynn was flattered. Jack must like her a lot.

"I hung on while he looked for it. The Paris boys did the rest. I'm sorry I can only stay until after lunch tomorrow . . ."

Lynn wasn't sure but she thought she felt a reaction from Clive.

". . . but I reckoned it'd be swell to see you. What do we do this evening? Are there any high spots?"

"I expect we can find something," Lynn answered looking forward to the evening.

They said cheerio to Clive and Jack hoped he'd have a good evening. "I noticed they'd got TV in the bar," he said to Lynn. "I was watching the football while I was waiting for you."

She had put on a light-coloured jacket that was ideal for evenings when she always felt she wanted something round her shoulders. "I expect Clive will look at it." She knew he liked the football. Then she wondered. What would he do? They hadn't thought to ask him to come along with them. But if they had, he would surely have refused. He'd been sitting in the lounge when they left, with the Continental edition of the newspaper Jack had brought from Paris.

Talking now and again but by no means over-talking Lynn and Jack walked along the promenade towards the harbour. "Not what you would call busy," Jack remarked and was surprised how small it was. "Is this the lot?"

He looked at the harbour and at the houses and shops and cafés rising from it and the lights of the few houses and hotels scattered along the high ground enclosing the bay.

He asked about her job, seeing it simply as a job, so that she told him it was going all right, and mentioned casually that Clive was working on it, too.

"Isn't it an odd job for a girl?"

She explained that it was a single, that she wasn't yet in business on her own.

"Likely you won't be. Isn't it about time you got married?"

Lynn laughed at his directness. "Yes . . . but there's no set time for taking that step."

He answered seriously as she might have expected. "No, but it must influence a woman's attitude to a career. You won't want to expend all that time and energy necessary to build up a business if you're going to pack it up for marriage."

"I could continue it after marriage."

"Not if you left the country."

Lynn smiled. "I hadn't thought of that." Had he?

It was another "moonlight and roses" night for atmosphere but it didn't lift Lynn into a world of its own. She was with Jack and was conscious of being herself. With Clive the other night there had been something of a dream quality.

This was preferable, because it was real. "I do appreciate your having come," she said impulsively.

"I'm pretty pleased myself," he grinned and looked round the café. A local girl had taken the floor and was doing a good version of the Flamenco.

"Pity the parents couldn't have come with me. They'd have enjoyed this. The simplicity of it. The real local colour. They'll not see anything like it on their trip."

Lynn agreed but was glad they hadn't!

Next morning she was up at her usual time and went to breakfast to find Clive waiting, but no Jack.

"We'll wait for him," she said and walked to the terrace door and stood looking out over the sea. It was another lovely morning. It was impossible to imagine East winds and frosts in England but she supposed you got used to anything. She'd be shocked now if she woke to anything but warmth and the sun rising on a deep blue sea!

"I hope you enjoyed yourself last evening." Clive's voice was pleasant but there was a reserved note in it as if the enquiry were polite rather than interested.

She nodded and was about to enlarge when she remembered last night and her thoughts about pink-shirt being a substitute waiter and all her uneasy thoughts about him since she had arrived.

"I know what I meant to tell you," she said and explained how she had noticed the man on her first evening when she thought he might have been light fingered and she had wondered about her personal possessions. "None has been touched, of course," she said half-apologetically. She was prepared for Clive to wipe aside her uneasiness as woman's bogies, mountains out of molehills and the rest.

He nodded and waited, and although his attitude gave her the go ahead it wasn't encouraging.

"The same man gave me our packed lunch yesterday." Clive's interest quickened.

"And he waited on us last night . . ."

"That clumsy fellow who had as much idea about waiting as a kangaroo?" Clive glared at her. "Why the heck didn't you tell me all this sooner?"

Lynn gaped then she flashed back, "Because it didn't happen altogether. It's the sum total that is interesting and because you are so full of your own ideas that you push mine aside as trivial . . ."

"For heaven's sake! How like a woman to rant. Take it calmly."

Lynn swallowed and, speechless, lifted her hand to smack his face when Jack's voice hailed her from the road. He had been on the beach before breakfast and was returning smiling and with a hearty appetite.

Pedro met his needs. "The bacon, the two eggs and the English toast."

Lynn turned to Jack with relief as Clive turned to their table and pulled up the chairs—that were already in position.

"I'm sorry I've got to go," Jack said, "but we have got the morning, Lynn. I leave after lunch. What's the programme?"

She'd been trembling after her words with Clive but as she drank her coffee her control returned and she answered Jack naturally. He deserved her attention . . . and her gratitude though he didn't know it. His arrival had prevented her losing her temper in a rough and tumble.

"I hadn't really thought. You haven't seen Flavidest in daylight . . ."

"Good enough." He took the idea in his straightforward way and talked about the harbour and the small, colourful spots of the Old World compared with the clean-cut distances of the New.

When they were at the far end of the harbour wall Lynn looked at the island

and felt convinced it could tell her something about Joan Tracey, and at the
thought she remembered Clive and his
scathing comments on her woman's
emotionalism and tried to dismiss the
feeling. It was facts she must follow not
fancies.

What was Clive doing? Working, of
course, but what at? Her eyes ranged along
the water front and she wondered if she'd
see his tall skinny figure. It would be easy
to pick out. He was mad at her for the way
in which she had withheld the information
about pink shirt—whose name was Marco
though he wasn't a Spaniard or an Italian,
Lynn was ready to swear—but that didn't
mean he would dismiss the information as
valueless. He had a check in himself. He
had remarked on the fact that Marco was
a clumsy waiter.

Jack and Lynn walked round the
harbour, talking about his parents' tour.
"They leave Paris tomorrow that's why
I've to leave here after lunch. How long
will you be staying?"

She shrugged.

"I was wondering if I might come down
again."

Lynn shook her head regretfully. "You might find I'd gone." So they talked about a meeting in London as soon as she returned.

From the harbour they walked up the narrow road that was little more than an alley, passed O'Connell's and at the top stood on the plateau and looked round the great bay of which Flavidest was a little cove.

Jack had brought a camera and Lynn made herself concentrate on him. She owed it to him to give him all the pleasure she could. Well, if she didn't exactly owe it to him because she hadn't asked him to come, she did want to please him. She laughed and enjoyed his company. He was so different from Clive. He had a pleasing knack of being interested in everything she showed him and of making comments that could not be misunderstood. There was never any need to wonder what was behind a remark!

Lynn pushed the dark hair off her face and saw Jack nod with approval—at her hair, not because he thought it had been in need of attention. If Clive had nodded like that she would immediately have known it had looked a mess before and probably wasn't much better now.

Jack talked about his work and reading between the lines she saw that he was restless when he was away from the job too long. He was enjoying this trip to Europe but having seen the Norwegian plant he was anxious to get back and work out possibilities for a similar installation.

He talked simply, not technically so that she could understand. He assumed her interest and made her feel that she was a woman and important—not in his man's world, but in his life.

He was ambitious and saw his goal that she knew he would achieve; he had a one track mind and saw so clearly along it.

"Your dad's a great guy," he said after he'd been telling her about some organisation behind the opening of a new venture.

"I know," she said warmly.

"You're like him. I don't know in what way. But you are. You're not like your mother."

Lynn raised her eyebrows but she didn't argue. Jack had formed his opinion. Actually she knew she had something of both parents, but she hoped she was more like

Dad. She'd like to acquire his width of vision, tolerance and good nature. She hadn't got it yet. She was inclined to be petty. She thought of her scrap with Clive this morning and saw it as a personal hitting out because her pride had been hurt. He had treated her as a child . . . Lynn bit her lip as she felt her resentment rising and turned to Jack, asking a laughing question, "Are you more like your mother or your father?"

After lunch which was a pleasant meal because Clive made an effort to be entertaining and obviously Jack found him so, Lynn and Jack sat in easy chairs in the sun to wait for his taxi.

Clive said goodbye to Jack. He was going out now and wouldn't be back before Jack left. He looked at Lynn, his eyes grey and level, and lifted his hand as he said, "Cheerio, I'll be seeing you."

"Not a bad fellow," Jack remarked and promptly forgot him. He'd never asked much about Clive, Lynn realised with a smile and she hadn't told him much. There really wasn't any need. "Bit of an actor."

He sat back and looked at the sea and

then sat up and looked into Lynn's face. "I shouldn't take too much notice of what he says."

"You wouldn't?" Lynn was surprised but managed to continue without a smile. "I—won't."

"Good."

The taxi came on time. Lynn was surprised but Jack wasn't. He had ordered it for this time.

She watched pink shirt—Marco—pack Jack's bags into the car and noticed he hung about to hear their farewells. He had had his tip.

"Goodbye," she said and gave Jack a friendly kiss. It couldn't be more in such public conditions.

"I'll see you," he said. "Let me know as soon as you are back in London." He kissed her again and got into the taxi.

"Thank you for coming," she said and added with a quick laugh, "I'd never be surprised to see you turn up anywhere at any time."

His coming had made a nice break. Now she must get back to work—and Clive. She felt herself stiffen. She wasn't going to find it easy to be natural with him. He didn't deserve that she should. She felt her hackles rising and breathed deeply to calm her feelings.

She was glad he'd gone out. She let out her breath and was grateful of the respite. It wouldn't be easy seeing him again without a third but it would be easier when she had had time to be objective about their relationship.

She crossed the road, and decided to walk along by the water's edge. It wasn't as calm as it had been. The wind had freshened and there were white horses out to sea.

Appreciatively Lynn strolled along and gradually her mood changed so she felt amused and almost ashamed of her words with Clive. What an opportunity she'd missed of behaving in a dignified manner.

Presently she found she was thinking of Joan Tracey and Charles Edgar. He sounded a thoroughly bad egg and she wondered what Joan had seen in him. Her compassion had been touched in the first place and then . . .

Lynn walked on, jumping from one to another of the few flat rocks that were a sudden outcrop in the beach. The sea was coming in in short rushes but she managed to avoid getting her feet wet.

At four o'clock she went to tea, composed and feeling able to be sensible with Clive. The best way was to behave naturally and take up the case in a businesslike manner.

Clive wasn't there; she waited until half past and then ordered. As she drank she wondered idly what he was doing and thought of Hendon's and the part they were playing from that end. Ellis had undoubtedly tapped all available sources of information. She didn't doubt that they had the true picture of Charles Edgar.

As the time passed Lynn's thoughts mellowed and she thought with quite happy anticipation of her meeting with Clive. It'd be rather fun to string him along. He had an attraction she found it hard to resist now that she wasn't in the office though he still got under her skin when he was so arrogant.

She thought of Jack, too, and her heart was warm. She was here on a job but that didn't mean she wasn't a young woman as well.

She dressed carefully for dinner and

after some thought pinned on Clive's brooch. She had felt illogically that she wouldn't wear it any more, not because of the strained relationship that might manifest itself between her and Clive, but because of Marco. It was illogical so she pinned it on her tangerine frock. Last time she'd worn the frock she'd felt glowing. As she looked at her reflection she saw the light in her eyes and the gold flecks in the green that meant she was excited.

She went to dinner soon after eight expecting to find Clive waiting for her as usual in the lounge.

She was surprised he wasn't there. He hadn't arrived by half past.

Marco came and looked at her and seemed to be waiting for her to go to dinner but she felt she couldn't move. Where was Clive? Had he come back from his afternoon's jaunt? She'd no means of knowing. He might be lying dead on his bedroom floor.

The picture terrified her so that she had the sense to pull herself together. What on earth was there to panic about? Clive wasn't really late.

But by nine o'clock he still hadn't come.

9

LYNN bit her lip and looked at her watch; it couldn't be nine o'clock already. But the lounge clock said the same. What on earth had happened to Clive? If he wasn't coming to dinner why hadn't he left a message?

She choked down her fears for his safety by letting her annoyance increase. If he were being late to avoid having a meal with her . . . ?

Lynn began to chew her thumb and then stopped abruptly, aware of what she was doing. She was getting jittery. If only she knew, if he were playing her up because of their scene, or if he were injured . . .

She slumped in the chair and tried to look at the book she'd found on one of the tables. She must stop staring at the door into the restaurant with the glazed look she could feel she was getting as the tension mounted in her.

She read deliberately but even so had no

163

idea what she was reading. Irritably she changed the book for a paper.

"Hallo."

She jumped, quite literally jumped, and because his entrance had frightened her she wanted to shout at him. It was Clive. She put aside the paper, unconcernedly she hoped. "Oh, hallo."

"I'm later than I expected. I hope you didn't wait dinner."

Lynn swallowed. He was exasperatingly off-hand. "I haven't had mine yet." How she wished she had.

"Cripes."

"It's all right. I wasn't . . . hungrily gnawing my nails."

He laughed politely. "Well, I'll only be a few minutes if you can hang on a bit longer. We might as well eat together as you haven't had yours."

"It's quite an idea," she agreed and her voice felt choked with temper.

She watched him walk upstairs, self-assured, master of his little world. How right she had been when she had judged he was impossible in the office. She found herself trembling and for a second she wanted to cry with relief that he was here.

164

She also wanted to shout at him, to let him know what she thought of his arrogance, his conceit and generally unattractive personality.

She saw Marco in the doorway and wondered how much he had seen and how much he had understood of what he had seen. A smile eased her irritated temper. They were behaving far more like a couple of tourists who were emotionally interested in one another than in colleagues on a job. It might be a good smoke screen. She saw Pedro and smiled.

"I'm sorry we're so late with dinner tonight, but Clive—Mr. Hendon—has only just got back."

He waved his hands, "I know, I saw the taxi and I tell the kitchen to make the specially good eggs while you have the soup."

Lynn's eyes lit up. She was hungry, and wondered how much hunger was the cause of her worry about Clive. If she hadn't been so—"polite"—but had eaten, she mightn't have felt any concern.

She smiled widely and felt that revelation had scaled Clive to size.

She heard the phone bell as she became

aware of Clive coming downstairs, quite unhurried.

"It is for you," Pedro indicated the phone and looked at her, to Clive and back again.

Lynn's natural instinct was to question. Was he sure? But her office training took her to the phone and she answered in a business like manner. "Lynn Laurel speaking."

There were gurgling noises the other end, then a man's voice came through, clear enough though it didn't sound as if it were in the next room. It wasn't. It was Jack phoning from Paris. He'd just got back to his hotel.

Lynn laughed. "I wondered who on earth it could be," she said and was aware that Clive was standing by her. She looked at him. What the dickens did he think he was doing? Was he trying to share the phone call with her?

"Is it Ellis?" he hissed. "Listen carefully . . ."

"What are you nattering about . . . No, not you, Jack. Wait just a minute. Clive seems to be in a bother about something." She put her hand over the phone. "You've

166

kept me waiting long enough. Now you can wait two minutes for me—and don't breathe down my neck." She uncovered the phone as Clive backed. "Sorry about that, Jack. How are you? Did you have a good flight? It's marvellous to hear your voice."

She heard his deep laugh and sensed that he was pleased with himself at her surprise. He'd phoned to thank her for a wonderful time. "It was good to see you."

"And you," Lynn said and knew that although she meant it, his words meant more than hers. He didn't make light conversation.

It was a short call but Lynn felt it did something to restore her self-respect. It compensated for Clive's indifference.

"Ready?" he asked, still as if time didn't matter.

Tomorrow will do, Lynn thought and felt her irritation threatening to rise, but she despatched it in amusement. Clive wasn't as nonchalant as he was trying to appear. Twice in three seconds he put his hands in his jacket pockets and took them out again, and as he let her precede him he put them in again.

They were alone on the terrace except for a French foursome who were finishing their dinner and preparing to leave.

Clive remarked on them, coupling it with his interest in the number of meals Pedro served. "The food is good."

Lynn let him make the conversation. She hoped she wasn't heavy. She was ready to follow any lead politely if not with enthusiasm.

Each was cool and as the meal progressed they developed the question and answer technique that served them well with Clive asking the questions. Towards the end Lynn asked some herself. Did he know if the TV here was live from a Spanish station or was it relayed? It was a good topic and lasted well.

Gradually Lynn felt a thaw and when Pedro put their coffee on the table Clive leaned forward as he helped himself to sugar and continued to sit in that position and speak quietly. "I went out this afternoon to phone Ellis about Marco. I thought it would be a good idea to find out if anything was known about the fellow."

He had followed his usual practice of going to a town where he wouldn't be known. It had been San Josédonet and he had had over an hour to wait for his call.

"I wasn't as lucky with the lines as I have been at other times." Lynn was about to commiserate when he continued, "But it's an attractive little place and I enjoyed sitting outside the post office watching the life of the people. The operator said he'd call me when the call was coming and he did." Clive lifted his head and his eyes looked directly into hers. "I've asked Ellis to check on Jack Delmore as well as Marco if you must know."

"There's no must about it," she answered crisply, and saw him wince as she raised her voice.

"If you've had enough coffee we might as well get out of here."

"A good idea," she agreed. "We must look silly whispering together when there's no one around to listen." She wasn't going to accept a rebuke from him.

They left the Miranda, crossed the road and leaned on the rail of the promenade, with their backs to the sea looking at the hotel.

Deciding that she wanted to be put in

the picture Lynn asked, "What information did you get from Ellis?"

"That the Boss is almost on his way. It was as I thought. Charles Edgar was released sooner than had been expected." He was silent for some seconds. "After what you told me about Marco . . ."

Lynn was suddenly conscious again of the scene that had caused the barrier between them and, remembering, stiffened. She felt Clive react and thought his voice was chilly as he continued.

". . . I wondered if he might be the Boss. I didn't think so. I think the fellow is an underling but naturally I wanted to check."

"Naturally," Lynn murmured.

"I've left his description with Ellis as far as it's apparent . . ."

"You mean he may be disguised?"

"What perspicuity," he murmured and Lynn bit her lip.

He cleared his throat almost apologetically as if the comment had slipped out and he wished it hadn't. "Also, I thought it right to check up on Jack Delmore." Clive's voice took on an aggressive note.

"He's a stranger to me. Ellis will report back."

"Quite," Lynn's voice was deliberately low-pitched. "I haven't known him long, but he is well-known to my father. I shall be interested to hear what information Ellis turns up."

Clive shot her a glance but didn't answer and Lynn found she'd nothing to say. They continued to lean on the promenade rail and look across the road at the lights of the Miranda, and in the silence something stirred between them. The sea was rolling in on the sand, with its soft swishing. To their right an accordion, accompanied by guitars, was playing some vibrant modern hits but because of the distance the music was stimulating to the senses rather than battering, and Lynn was conscious that a quiet appreciation of the night was taking possession of her.

It was beautiful whoever the companion. It had something of its own to give . . .

Clive cleared his throat again and Lynn's interest quickened.

"Would you like to go out somewhere? I wondered if you'd like to go along and . . . er . . . enjoy the night life. I thought we might call in at O'Connell's for about half an hour."

"It sounds a good idea," she replied simply, and ten minutes later they were walking up the alley. Dan O'Connell made them welcome but they learned nothing and later went to the café dance-bar of the hotel on the plateau.

Clive was subdued, Lynn thought and his politeness wasn't coldly strained and assumed. It seemed part of a pleasant wish to be . . . well, pleasant. She felt herself responding. Perhaps there was some magic in the night?

They were still talking of the job. Lynn gave him the lead and he told her how he thought the situation might develop. "It's only guesswork," he said, almost humbly, "but I'm more convinced than ever that when the Boss turns up so will Charles Edgar." They still called him Charles Edgar though his real name, as Clive had told Lynn, was Charles Dawson. "I believe he is avoiding being seen in this district. Naturally secrecy is the essence of such a business."

Lynn nodded.

"I suppose the fellow thinks he can go

on where he left off. I should have thought the Boss would have found someone to take his place. But it's impossible to see into the workings of his mind, of course. It's all guess."

"Of course." Lynn had no wish to be sarcastic though a few hours ago she wouldn't have been able to resist the opportunity.

"I wonder if he'll bring Joan with him when he comes?" Clive murmured.

"If he does, what do we do?" Lynn asked.

Clive shook his head, then said slowly, "I suppose we try and get her alone and talk to her. I don't think we can tell her who and what Charles Edgar is. I think we must try and get her to go back home first." He looked at her. "Do you think you'll be able to persuade her to go home and sort things out with her parents?"

"I've no idea," Lynn answered. She'd never met Joan Tracey. All she knew she'd learned secondhand. "I should think everything hangs on her feelings for Charles Edgar. If this, if that." It was like trying to see over a high brick wall, she thought, and when you got a peek over there were brambles and briars on the other side.

They returned to the Miranda in the early hours and as they entered the lounge found Pedro waving. "Ah—si—the good time—just."

There was a call for Miss Laurel. The young man had rung before. Jack? Lynn asked as she hurried to the phone.

"Lynn Laurel speaking," she said automatically. Even with her brain asking who and what, her office training stood.

"Lynn . . . I'm a boy-friend. Act it. Ellis here . . ."

"Oh, how marvellous of you to ring," she gasped and instinctively she was alert to the seriousness of the situation. "How wonderful to hear your voice."

"Good girl," was the grunted reply. "Boss on his way tomorrow. Aim to kill . . ." he paused.

She giggled. "Go on."

". . . kill Charles Edgar."

"How sweet of you to have phoned." Lynn felt as if her brain was going numb under the impact of his news and braced herself.

"The grapes are good," he said.

"That's wonderful. I'll be glad to see you too . . ." She felt as if she was beginning to gabble. "You're sure you're well?"

"I'm certain of what I've told you."

"I'll . . . I mean . . ." She felt suddenly dumb.

"Love and kisses," Ellis prompted.

"Me, too . . . Love and kisses. You're a darling."

There was a click at the other end and Lynn put down the phone with a trembling hand.

"Another of your boy-friends," Clive grunted, winked at Pedro, and taking her arm held it firmly as he led her out of the Miranda and across the road to the promenade rails. Lynn leaned against them thankfully. She wouldn't have got across the road without Clive's support.

Slowly she drew in a deep breath in an effort to stop trembling. They were back where they had been after dinner this evening.

"Take it easy. I suppose it was Ellis? The news will keep for five minutes. Do you need a coffee?"

"No."

Clive lit a cigarette and leaned back with

every appearance of being out to enjoy a last smoke before turning in.

"It was Ellis."

"I guessed. Sorry I hadn't warned you that when he rang he was going to ask for you, boy friend fashion. I didn't expect any gen until tomorrow. That call was trouble, wasn't it?"

Lynn told him what Ellis had said, that the Boss was coming for the purpose of killing Charles Edgar.

Clive gave a soundless whistle.

"He said something about the grapes being good."

"He means the news is reliable. It came by the grapevine but is more than rumour. Er . . . thanks for playing your part so well, Lynn."

"What do we do now?" Her voice was sober.

"Hanged if I know. I wonder if Charles Edgar had some inkling of the situation, so hasn't come here to meet the Boss but to get away from him? I wonder if the Boss has tracked him here and is going to winkle him out of hiding?"

Lynn shivered.

"It's a switch round. But it isn't unusual

in our job, to be following what seems to be a direct clue and find it's taking you in circles and revealing something unexpected."

They were standing close together so that Lynn could feel his sleeve against her arm.

"I wonder . . . I wonder if your hunch about the island is a lead? Joan and that fellow could be in hiding there."

It was possible, Lynn agreed, but felt too weary to think reasonably. She was tired and knew she wouldn't be able to follow any thought to its logical conclusion.

Her mind was refusing to take any more of the case and she was aware vaguely, but with a background happiness, of moonlight and roses. Moonlight and roses in March. She smiled at the sentimentality of the phrase but it held some truth. It was a moonlight night and there were roses . . .

"You're tired," his voice broke her thoughts and she realised she had yawned.

For a second she panicked, fearing he might take offence and slip back into his cold politeness but he put his arm round her shoulders. "Tomorrow will do," he said.

They waited for a car then crossed to the hotel. It was still awake. If a customer arrived he would be welcomed and a meal placed before him, but there was an air of the end-of-the-day about. The coloured lights of the terrace were switched off as Clive and Lynn walked up the steps and there was only one man on duty in the bar. He said goodnight, in Spanish, and went on talking to a man at the counter.

"It's as late as we've been," Clive yawned.

Lynn nodded. Tiredness had come on her suddenly and now she felt too tired even to talk. They walked upstairs in silence but it was a friendly absence of speech.

Lynn rather felt as if she were walking on clouds in a woolly atmosphere. She thought she would be asleep as soon as her head touched the pillow. She turned to Clive, and froze.

His arm had shot round her and was drawing her into the shadows of a recess. Marco was going along the corridor, ahead of them walking silently.

Clive's arm was firm and Lynn received its support gratefully as her sleepy senses came to life with a jerk. She was alert to Marco's presence—and to Clive's proximity.

He gave a low chuckle. Marco shut the window at the end of the passage and turned to come back. Clive thrust Lynn upright but kept his arm round her as he propelled her forward and bent his head towards hers in a loving attitude.

With simulated surprise he saw Marco and moved slightly to let him pass. Marco turned down a back staircase.

Outside her door Lynn found her key and fumbled to open it. Her senses were tumbling over one another in an excited frenzy.

Clive took the key, unlocked her door and stood for a moment looking down at her. His eyes were blue grey tonight.

"Goodnight," he said and putting out his hand let it rest on her shoulder and then run down her arm to give her fingers a little squeeze.

"Goodnight," her voice was a whisper. "Goodnight."

10

GOING upstairs Lynn had felt so tired that she had imagined she would be asleep as soon as her head settled in the pillow. Now she undressed with her mind fully awake and her feelings beset by uneasiness. She wasn't afraid. She had locked the door and Clive's room was next to hers. She wasn't sure what comfort that was, but she was glad he wasn't along another passage.

She got into bed and lay still. Somehow she had to come to terms with her feelings and accept the fact that she had to live through the night, and that it would be more sensible to sleep than to lie awake.

How reasonable, she thought and tried to direct her mind to Jack and his thoughtfulness in ringing to say he'd enjoyed himself. She had enjoyed his company . . .

Was Marco really shutting the window? Was it necessary for it to be shut? It was a warm night and there was little wind.

She frowned and tried to see Marco's

face in her mind's eye. Was there anything to tell her anything? She shook her head. He looked neither rogue nor saint but rather a flesh-loving man in his middle thirties, inclining to weightiness and therefore possibly lazy.

She thought of Ellis and wondered if he would be able to discover anything. Hendon's had an efficient network of agents but it wouldn't be easy to pick up anything about Marco on the slender information Clive had been able to give.

From Ellis her thoughts went to Clive and suddenly something pent-up in her was released.

She was glad he was at the Miranda. She admitted that without a stop in her mind, but because sleep seemed so far away she began rationalising. It was natural she should feel gratitude. She couldn't have tackled the job alone. As much as he annoyed her personally and they seemed to rub each other the wrong way, she admitted he was an able colleague . . . and could make himself an attractive companion.

She lay very still as she relived those moments in the corridor recess when he had pulled her to him. Lynn's heart beat suffocatingly. She could feel the hot air, the thin strength of his arm.

She turned, seeking a cool place on the pillow and directed her mind to Jack. What a difference. It was a happy compliment his flying down to see her. She couldn't imagine Clive doing anything like that. Her breath caught in her throat. Of course he wouldn't. He wasn't in love with her.

Was Jack? Lynn didn't think so—not yet.

Was she in love with him? Not yet.

She admitted the possibility. Neither had bowled the other over but there was something that pulled them towards each other. His work was predominant in his life, or had been. He spoke as if he were ready to settle down, but wasn't he too restless? Supposing he were offered a job on a five year project? He had talked, as if it wouldn't concern him personally, about switching over some of the firm's work to the Norwegian type of plant.

Mother hadn't taken to Jack. Dear mother. Lynn laughed to herself. Away on her own she was able to see more clearly and to appreciate even while she freed herself from her mother's apron strings. The old-fashioned phrase! But it was still a true one. She had been too lazy to live her own life and follow her "own devices". She had always thought tomorrow would do.

The thought reminded her of Joan Tracey and she experienced a sense of guilt. She had come out here to find Joan, not to work out her own emotional growing-up.

The situation was much worse than she had imagined it would be. How much did Joan know? Charles Edgar was not only an ex-convict, he was a bigamist and seemingly was prepared to go back into the racket for which he received his prison sentence. He sounded a rotten egg. Were there any good parts?

She thought of the Boss and Ellis's news that he was out to kill Charles Edgar. It sounded too sensational. On the other hand there was big money in drug running . . .

Lynn was pondering on the motive power of money when she became aware of a quiet scuffling. It was so slight that she dismissed it, then her senses quickened. It sounded almost as if someone was on the balcony. She grew taut and wasn't sure if she could hear anything or not.

Finally, convinced she could, her instinct was to lie still, in an ostrich-like faith that she would not be seen if anyone came into her room. Then her feelings steadied and she began to wonder. If someone was on the balcony, what had they come for? Was the intruder aiming to break into her room? He would have to open the shutter.

Lynn sat up. It was a defiant gesture, born more of desperation than courage. She couldn't lie there all night in a state of fear. She was damp round the forehead and along her upper lip, and her hands felt clammy. If anything was going to happen she might as well precipitate it.

But she didn't make a noise. She got out of bed, walked silently to the window and peered out between the slats of the shutter. There was no one on her balcony.

Nevertheless she felt someone. Pressing her forehead against the shutter she looked as far to the right as she could manage and saw a form. A man was on Clive's balcony, standing back against Clive's window, smoking.

Lynn stood up with a smile and a warm feeling round her heart as her fear dropped away. It was Clive. He couldn't sleep either, she guessed, so he was standing outside having a cigarette. Still smiling she jumped into bed and went straight to sleep.

Next morning the sun was shining, and Lynn thought there was a feeling of exhilaration in the air.

Clive was waiting in the lounge and as they went to breakfast Pedro gave them a pleasant welcoming, "Good day." They were lucky he went on. "Not often are we so fortunate at this time of the year. It is usual for the winds. They will come." He waved his hands and Lynn smiled her appreciation as Clive answered in Spanish and Pedro replied in his own tongue.

"How did you sleep?" Clive asked as they chose a table.

Lynn looked at him with searching eyes. She couldn't explain but in some way she had expected him to look different this morning. He was himself—nonchalant, pleasant, and he looked as he always did —bright and self-assured.

She realised he was waiting for a reply and that his eyes on her had sharpened. "I didn't get off to sleep quickly," she admitted, "but I slept soundly when I did. What about you?" How long had he stayed on the balcony?

"I didn't get off straight away," he replied. "I found I had some thinking to do."

Lynn nodded. "Did your thoughts get you anywhere?"

Again his eyes sharpened and he shook his head, but not very certainly. "I'm not sure," he admitted. He sat back to let Marco put the hot rolls on the table and his eyes followed the man's clumsy movements. His raised eyebrows told Lynn his thoughts now.

Before they went out, Clive had a word with Pedro. As she was coming downstairs to join him she heard him talking and heard Pedro laugh and she looked from one to the other curiously.

"I do not believe it," Pedro told her. "He tells me he is not the favourite with you."

Lynn shot Clive a look.

"He says that you have the other specials. One in London . . ."

"I was telling Pedro that you are expecting another call from London."

Lynn nodded, "That is so," and she hoped she looked happier than she felt. Though of course, Clive knew Ellis wasn't a boy friend. Lynn brightened.

"Ready?" he asked and they walked out in friendly fashion. What did Pedro think? Lynn wondered. Surely Pedro must think there was something odd in their relationship?

She wasn't given time to pursue her thoughts along that interesting line. Clive wanted to talk.

"It's no good wondering what news Ellis will get for us, but I confess I'll be glad to know. Have you noticed all cases tend to take the same pattern?"

Lynn shook her head. She wasn't experienced.

"They do by and large. First it's all go as you plunge into a case. Avenues appear to be there for the following and you rush up them. Then it's deadlock."

This time Lynn nodded. That's where

they were now. Was that where she was in herself? She admitted she was wondering what would happen next in her private life, and she admitted she was expectant.

"In this period," Clive was saying, "you wonder what the other fellow is doing. You see him as active and try to imagine the way his mind is working." His brow furrowed. "Then there is the third and last phase when things happen, often suddenly and from the least considered angle, and wham you're in it, up to your neck."

The amusement showed in Lynn's eyes and Clive smiled back, but he defended his words. "We are waiting. Something will explode somewhere soon."

"Do you really think the Boss will try to kill Charles Edgar?"

"I think he's coming here, with that intention. Hendon's don't know the man so we don't know if he has the nerve: It's unlikely, I should say. Men do kill, but the majority who get on the wrong side of the law aren't killers . . . unless for vengeance or because there's an awful lot of money involved." He lifted his head. "Or because they're afraid, of course."

Lynn thought Clive was casual about the

possibility of Charles Edgar's murder but realised he was doubtful of the Boss's intentions.

As they sat on a seat facing the harbour he briefed her about Ellis's call. "It should come through some time today. I've told him when we're in for meals so he'll try and catch us then."

Lynn's eyes clouded. "It's not easy to talk as if . . . if I'm in love with him."

"Think it's Jack."

"Don't be silly," she snapped flushing and saw him bite his lower lip. "Why didn't you ask Ellis to get Irene to phone and then you could have put on an act that she was your girl friend?"

Lynn felt the harmony fading between them and was disappointed but she had flared instinctively at his quip about Jack. Naturally he thought Jack was her boy friend. A casual acquaintance wouldn't fly from Paris for three quarters of a day.

Lynn felt herself drifting into realms of conjecture. Suppose the positions were reversed? Supposing a girl had flown from —say Brussels to see Clive? She'd have said she was chasing him. Lynn chuckled and brought herself back to the present.

"You didn't suggest Irene, so I'll have to do my best."

"Yes." There was no argument.

"If only I knew what to talk about." Lynn sighed. It wasn't an easy act to put on.

Clive was ready. "When you've expressed your surprise at another phone call . . ."

"You told Pedro I was expecting one."

"Cripes, so I did. Well, when you've expressed your joy you can say how much you're looking forward to seeing him again, flirt a bit. But don't be so intent on your act that you miss what he is saying."

The idea amused Lynn and they both laughed so that the threatened disharmony disappeared.

"Now," he said in a businesslike fashion that was typical but not very impressive because he looked so relaxed, "we've to think about Joan Tracey. She's our chief concern today."

Lynn thought how she would have to face up to a terrible shock in the near future. Did she know why Charles Edgar had gone to prison? Clive had said only minor charges could be proved against him.

"I wish we could get her away before the fun starts."

"Kidnap her?" Lynn's eyes lit up.

"It's an idea," he agreed and thought about it. "She's the innocent party so it might be a good move."

"Does the Boss know anything about Joan?"

Clive shrugged. "The marriage was kept pretty dark. I heard of it by . . . luck." He looked up at the sky. "I wonder where the Boss is now?" There were very few planes about at any time.

They talked. And talked. Lynn agreed when Clive said waiting was a drag.

"What about a boat trip?" he asked at last.

Again Lynn's eyes lit up but before she could reply a shadow fell across their feet and Guan was with them. She knew a moment's irritation but Clive welcomed the interruption.

"Hello," he said cheerily and began talking in Spanish. Then he turned to Lynn laughing. "That's rude of me, but I can't resist the opportunity of trying out my skill."

Guan smiled widely at Lynn, "I am always glad to see my friend Clive and his lady."

Lynn bit her lip and held back a laugh of denial as she remembered that in spite of the phone calls from "boy friends" she was Clive's lady friend on this trip. She looked at Clive and on seeing that he looked embarrassed a smile lit her eyes.

But in spite of his embarrassment he was still in charge of the situation and asked Guan about a boat. "What about the island? Can we go there?"

Eagerly Lynn waited for the reply.

"I see," Guan nodded. "I make arrangements that are good for your pocket. Guan is your friend." He didn't find English easy but was careful to use it when he spoke to them both.

He went off and in six or seven minutes was back. "Me, I fix it. Follow."

Clive gave Lynn his hand to pull her to her feet. "This is good tourist stuff. It's the sort of jaunt that is popular, and we might learn something. Keep your eyes on the island. Pity we haven't binoculars, but

I'll use the camera." He spoke quickly as Guan waved to them to come along. "We might work out the possibility of kidnapping Joan." They walked swiftly to the boat Guan had hired. It was red and blue outside and all white in, so Clive brought his camera into play. "It's a pity your frock is white but the green sandals will look good."

They sat aft while Guan joined the boatman and took the wheel as they cast off. Gently the small boat chugged forward and then the owner took over, speed increased and they turned seawards.

The wind blew the hair back from Lynn's forehead although it had seemed so calm ashore and she saw that Clive's fair hair was standing up, and immediately they were clear of the harbour they could feel the pull of the current and the dip of the boat to the tide. Lynn drew in a deep breath and enjoyed the feeling that comes with being on the sea.

Guan came to Clive and now he spoke in Spanish. Lynn tautened and for a moment wondered if they had walked into a trap. If Marco were the Boss's man it was possible they were suspect and so it would be expedient to remove them. And this was the means. But Clive was nodding and presently took some money from his pocket and it changed hands.

Lynn sighed her relief, amazed how quick she was to suspect. Guan had bargained for this trip for them, and obtained favourable terms, Clive told her in an amused voice, "with a fair commission for himself, no doubt."

The island was farther away than it looked from the shore and they had been going for twenty minutes before it appeared appreciably nearer.

Clive questioned Guan on its size and distance from the mainland as he adjusted his camera and took some shots. "What is it used for?"

Guan shrugged and giving her an apologetic glance Clive continued his questioning in Spanish. Guan's replies were voluble, but Clive didn't learn much of value. At one time there had been a few families on the island his grandfather had told him, but the living was too poor and the sheep had not flourished, and in the Summer there was almost no water. "But the birds are glad."

As the island came fully into view Lynn saw this land side was rocky with stunted trees and scrub growing among the boulders. There was a sandy cove at which it would be possible to land a boat, with a narrow stone jetty that was part of the rocks. And what had appeared as a broken down habitation from the telescope on the plateau was certainly derelict looking on nearer sight.

The sea side seemed to be sheer rock with the waves breaking against a rugged shore and sea birds swirling and circling.

Lynn watched fascinated, eager that Clive should use his ciné. "It'll be wonderful in colour with the sea beating up like that and the spray. Will the rainbow come out?"

"I don't see why not." He was standing braced against the wind and the movement of the small boat.

In the midst of her enjoyment Lynn remembered the object of their trip and scanned the island for a possible hideout. She saw there were caves inland where the land rose in diagonal lines of rocky strata but none looked inhabited.

Where were Joan and Charles Edgar?

11

THE boat trip back to Flavidest was a delight to Lynn. She leaned over the side and trailed her hand in the water, watching the wavelets run back. The whole trip had been a delight. Flavidest was a wonderful out of the way holiday centre—but she didn't think it would suit mother.

All Lynn wanted to do was let her mind wander and appreciate the day, but Joan Tracey was at the back of her mind, and Joan was the reason for her being here. It wasn't a happy situation. Once they had located Joan, Lynn knew her hardest task would begin. She tried to imagine how Joan would react to the news of Charles Edgar's illegal activities if she didn't know about them. It puzzled her. Unless Joan were besotted surely she must have some idea what Charles Edgar was like? A drug trafficker and a bigamist. It wasn't a pretty combination.

Her eyes were seriously dark as she

196

stared into the water. Charles Edgar was a bad egg but Clive couldn't let him be killed in cold blood. His task was far more difficult than hers.

She looked at him and wondered what he was thinking. Although the island had fallen well behind now he was still looking at it with his camera to his eye.

She wished she had a camera. He'd make a good picture standing braced against the movement of the boat with his fair hair, light navy shirt, off-white slacks and the background of the blue-green sea.

Charles Edgar was Clive's concern. Had the ex-convict a meeting arranged with the Boss? She guessed he had and thought how easy it would be for her and Clive to miss it. They hadn't a clue who the Boss was.

For the first time, Lynn wondered if they really had been wasting their time. Supposing Clive's hopes in Dan O'Connell were misplaced? She turned from staring into the water and blinked as she tried to re-focus her eyes.

"What's up?" Clive was watching her.

"The sea's dazzling."

"It's the way the sun glints back.

Here . . ." He took off his sun specs. "Try mine. They don't take out the colour." He sat beside her talking of nothing very much.

"There's good fishing on the south-west of the island."

"Is there?" Lynn looked past the island and was aware of his arm against hers as it had been in the corridor last night. She sat taut and then deliberately made herself relax.

With a wide sweep the boatman took them into the harbour and with a shout of triumph brought them alongside the steps. Guan cheered as well and Clive grinned as he helped Lynn ashore and they all parted with wide smiles and a babble of goodbyes.

Lynn laughed and felt for a moment as if her legs didn't belong to her. She was swaying with the movement of the boat. At least she thought it must be that. She looked at Clive disbelievingly. He couldn't be doing this to her.

In a daze she followed him to a shop to buy cards. "We must keep up our tourist image," he was saying and gave her a sudden, sharp look. "Are you all right? You don't feel seasick do you?"

"No."

"It's not the sun?"

She made herself laugh. She was sure it wasn't.

She chose a card for her mother and every now and again looked at Clive in a wondering manner. When he was out of sight, round the other side of the shop, her eyes sought him.

This was ridiculous. He was getting under her skin—if he hadn't already got there.

On their unhurried walk back to the Miranda Lynn was conscious of her feelings. Her very real liking for Clive was rooted in admiration, she told herself. She admired the way he was handling this case —even when she thought that he was doing next to nothing? she asked herself realistically, and gave up the struggle of rationalising. Clive had got under her skin . . . and it felt very much as if she was falling in love with him.

That was it. She was more than half in love with him. It made her feel faint.

He was talking of the island. "It seems

uninhabited and obviously there have been no rumours of anyone landing there and staying—at any rate recently. Guan wouldn't have been able to resist using the idea as a tourist attraction."

Lynn agreed. Clive was subdued, she thought. He was self-confident but he wasn't his usual aggressive self. In some way he seemed more tolerant. It could be that his usual exuberance was dampened by the tragedy threatening the case. She didn't think he was depressed or worried. He was certain Flavidest was the centre for the case and she believed he was sure that when things began to move he would be on to them. Was it arrogant conceit? It could be he didn't know the Boss or Charles Edgar.

"It's pretty obvious Joan and Charles Edgar aren't there," he was saying.

"Then how on earth do you think you can do anything in the case?" she burst out.

He drew in a deep breath. "I'm sure of Flavidest. I'm sure greed is the motive power in Charles Edgar's life. I'm sure he won't be able to resist getting back into the game for the big money."

"Go on."

"I'm sure the Boss is coming here."

"So?"

Clive stared straight ahead. "Charles Edgar will come here to meet him and pick up the threads of his old life. The Boss probably imagines he'll be too dangerous a colleague. With a prison sentence he could be a marked man in the Boss's eyes."

"How will you know the Boss?"

"I'm relying on Ellis's being able to give us a description—and possibly some idea of the rendezvous. I believe we'll learn from O'Connell when Joan and Edgar are here."

Lynn absorbed the information. Clive had had three talks with Ellis and Hendon's file had been well authenticated before Clive left London.

"I'll be glad to get back," she burst out.

"Jack?" he asked raising his eyebrows.

"No . . . I'll be glad to be out of the case." The words burst from her and she waited for a sarcastic reply. She had walked into it with open eyes.

"I can understand that," he said, gently. "It's not a job for a woman. I'd suggest your going home now only there's Joan Tracey to think of. She'll need you."

They walked in silence and Lynn marvelled at his understanding.

Pedro greeted them with smiles. "You have enjoyed the trip round the island?"

Clive looked at him with suddenly narrowed eyes.

"Guan has been in and we hear all about it . . ."

Lynn saw Clive relax and assure Pedro they had enjoyed the trip very much.

"He is planning another, down the coast for you, past the artist's colony . . ."

"We're not staying here for a month," Clive protested and asked Lynn what she would like to drink before lunch.

As she turned to one of the lounge chairs she saw Marco in the far doorway and caught the expression in his eyes. They were suddenly staring and then he drew back and disappeared.

Lynn put out her hand and finding Clive's gripped it convulsively. Startled he looked at her and then looked towards the doorway. It was empty. He sat beside her and continued to let her hold his hand. For a moment she let her feelings rule, then she tried to think. What had made her react so violently? She couldn't say his expression was evil.

She turned to Clive and shook her head apologetically as she released his hand and picked up her drink. She sipped it with her head bent, still trying to understand why she had reacted as she had. It was unreasonable. But she was feeling unreasonable. It wasn't reasonable to be in love with Clive.

As they went to lunch Clive looked round. "We'll have a different table," he said and Lynn knew with a throb of relief he had seen Marco even if he had not seen the expression on his face. He chose the table at which Pedro's youngest son usually served, under the eye of his father.

He took their order then Clive talked casually. Lynn put her hand to her forehead, pushed back the hair and then let her fingers stray to the shoulder of her frock. She wasn't wearing the brooch.

"You haven't lost it, have you?" Clive asked. "You were wearing it this morning."

"No." Lynn hesitated and then opened her handbag and took it out, not in its box but wrapped in a tissue. "I'm not having it lost," she averred and she smiled when she saw the look of pleasure cross his face. She went on, because it was a happy subject, to explain that she had not worn it when she put on a cardigan on the boat. "Sometimes the setting pulls a thread."

They talked quietly. She told him she never left it in her bedroom. "It's not really that I think it might be stolen but . . ." she smiled into his eyes, ". . . I'm not risking it."

For once he seemed speechless.

Lynn was beginning to wonder if she could think of another topic of conversation when the phone rang and she saw Clive tense and then nod as Pedro came towards them. "Ellis is on time," he said and his relaxed expression gave way to an alert wariness. "You'll be all right. Whatever you do, listen. I'll cover up this end if you talk gibberish. Remember they don't understand English all that well—I hope."

Pedro came laughing and shaking his head. It was a call for Miss Laurel. He raised his eyebrows at Clive and Lynn wondered what he really thought. Probably being a hotel proprietor he was used to queer relationships.

"Come along," Clive held out his hand and as if it were the most natural thing in the world he walked to the phone with her. If you did anything naturally enough it disarmed criticism, "Thanks," she breathed under her breath. "Do what you like, tease me, say something."

He grinned and talked in his natural voice about the inconsideration of some men in phoning at a time that spoilt other people's meals. He praised the Miranda cuisine.

"Hallo, yes?" Lynn spoke into the phone. She was trembling and fearful she wouldn't be able to hear. For one wild second she hoped it would be Jack's voice and this would truly be a boy friend's call.

"Ellis here . . ."

She braced herself. "Oh darling . . ."

"Ready? There's nothing on Marco."

"That's wonderful." Lynn meant it. It was only later that Clive pointed out that didn't mean he wasn't working for the Boss. "You are sweet to phone again so soon."

"There's nothing on Jack Delmore."

"Oh—lovely."

"The Boss is on his way. Charles Edgar's life is in danger."

"Yes, it's seemed a long time to me, but I will soon be back."

"That has been confirmed from a most reliable source."

"I'm not quite sure which day it will be but I'll be sure to let you know. Don't be possessive," Lynn spoke poutingly.

"Have you got it clear? The Boss is a killer."

"Yes, I know it must have seemed a long time . . . and I love you, too." She heard Clive catch his breath and wished she hadn't said those words but she was running out of conversation. With relief she heard Ellis grunt.

"Good girl," and the phone clicked dead.

"Goodbye darling. See you soon," she said in a strong voice, and turned to face Clive. Her forehead was wet and her body felt damp but she was exhilarated. She'd done her job and thought she had done it well.

Clive was putting on an act, for Pedro in the café doorway. "A bird in the hand is worth two in the bush," he grinned as he took Lynn's hand.

Pedro frowned and there followed a hilarious five minutes while Clive translated.

Pedro's son served them efficiently and at speed. Their half-finished course had been whisked away and fresh placed before them.

Lynn looked round. Marco wasn't on duty.

As if he read her thoughts Pedro told them Marco had gone. "He was the no good waiter."

Lynn smiled and the smile reached her eyes but she saw that Clive was puzzled as he listened to Pedro.

"It was good the way it turned out that pleased me. He was the no good waiter as I see from the first meal he serve and I think to make myself give him the sack. But to my joy, he sack himself, and we shake the hands, the good friends still."

Clive nodded and asked why Pedro had employed him.

"He want the job. It is early in the season, I can afford to try him, and he did not ask the high wages."

Lynn met Clive's eyes. Ellis might not have learned anything about Marco but she had no doubt, and neither had Clive as he admitted when they were leaning on the promenade rail later, that Marco was here with a purpose that wasn't waiting.

Lynn reported her conversation with Ellis. "He was absolutely sure. The Boss is a killer. He made sure I understood." She looked up at Clive. "What makes him think he will get away with murder?"

Clive looked round and Lynn imagined that in his mind's eye he was seeing the wild, craggy scrubland round Flavidest. "Why does any man think he will get away with it—when it's planned? Crimes of sudden violence come in a different category. They're not premeditated . . . in the same way. They may be the result of a dream of hate." He fell silent.

"Ellis said that the Boss is actually on his way."

"Ah. Action stations. He will arrive this evening probably. Ellis didn't give you any description I suppose?"

"No."

"Never mind. I wonder if Joan and Charles Edgar are in Flavidest yet?"

Lynn had no thoughts to offer. She felt numb and wished with a deep longing that she were at home. On the other hand she wouldn't want to be at home without Clive. She looked at him and found herself moving closer. He noticed, she felt his awareness, but he didn't look at her.

They spent the afternoon sitting in the sun watching the activity round the harbour. "Er . . ." Lynn immediately detected the different note in Clive's voice. "Did Ellis say anything about Jack Delmore?"

Lynn laughed. "I'm sorry. I forgot. No. I mean yes."

He looked at her and Lynn felt he thought she was confused because of her feelings for Jack and she would have liked to kick herself. "What I'm trying to say is that there is nothing on Jack."

"I didn't really think there would be, but I had to check. You understood that, didn't you?"

"Of course."

"I'm sure he's a grand fellow."

Don't, she wanted to shout, and found herself wallowing in her own situation rather than keeping a clear mind to go along with Clive in speculating when things would begin to happen. Naturally Clive thought she was interested in Jack.

"What about some tea?" he asked and they went to an outside café where the roses had come out fully during the last few days and were scenting the air.

It was quietly peaceful and Lynn felt every moment was precious. Clive was attentive and there was something in his manner that she knew was in tune with her feelings. It was as if he wanted to please.

After tea they went to O'Connell's. "If we don't get news of Joan and Edgar there I'll have miscalculated," Clive said and Lynn knew that he was edgy now that the time for action was coming. He said he had no "cut and dried" plan and she believed him. He would have to cope with situations as they arose. First he must have solid news of Joan and Charles Edgar. She fancied his plan was to put Joan in her charge and then deal with the position— but how? She knew a swift uprush of panic but daren't say anything. Whatever happened she wasn't going to leave Clive.

They went to the Miranda, checked there had been no more phone calls for

Lynn, with Clive playing his facetious part, and then, when Lynn had fetched a cardigan, they strolled off. The Western sun would soon give way to evening. The lights of the shops and café were on and the street lights. From the front they turned into the narrow alley.

They walked hand in hand, each lost in private thoughts. Lynn guessed Clive's were on the business on hand. That was probably why he had been quiet this afternoon. Hers were on him, and on the way her heart lurched when she looked at him and she felt the blood race when he took her hand and his arm touched hers.

Suddenly his grip tightened and she became aware of a figure turning down the alley that crossed theirs.

"Marco," Clive breathed, his pace quickening and Lynn knew he was excited. The time for waiting was almost over. Marco had come from O'Connell's. She felt sick inside.

Dan O'Connell was pleased to see them "Greetings, my friends." He nodded and gave them their usual Sangria, mixing it himself and talking as he did so. He was always talkative but seemed more so than usual this evening. There were a few other customers and Lynn looked at them curiously, but none resembled Joan or Charles Edgar. None was English.

Dan drank with them. "My brother is coming today," he remarked and nodded to the doorway as if he could see his brother's form. Then he looked at Clive as if he would recognise the importance of the information.

Clive nodded looking into his drink. "Does he often come for a visit?"

"Not what you might call often considering what a beautiful spot this is."

"If I had a brother here I should want to fly out pretty often."

"It suits me . . ." Dan's voice faded and Lynn saw him looking at Clive and then at her. "And it's my guess you think it suits you, too."

"We do indeed." Clive took Lynn's hand and did his happy tourist act, as Lynn was coming to call it with distaste.

"I've been thinking of your friends . . ."

"Yes?" Clive's manner was casually interested.

"They were interested in the island."

"We took out a boat and circled it today."

"You did now?"

Clive nodded and looked at Lynn as if remembering that it had been fun. They exchanged looks and laughed.

"That's right, my dears," Dan said and his brogue became more noticeable. "Go to the harbour long arm tomorrow at ten-thirty."

Lynn felt relief flood her because Clive had got his news. She had been half-fearful he was on the wrong track, and felt she wouldn't have been able to bear his disappointment. Now at least he knew. She forgot the possible danger for a moment and relaxed against the double seat where they were sitting. The room was filling and Dan had to attend other customers.

Clive and Lynn were sitting quietly, hardly talking, but there was no feeling of restraint. Lynn realised that had been absent for a long time now. There might be coolness, irritation, temper but there wasn't restraint. The difference between coolness and restraint was difficult to define but she satisfied herself by thinking of coolness as a lack of warmth that could

213

easily be overcome and restraint a clash of personalities that was rooted in real antagonism!

"What's amused you?" Clive asked.

"I was rationalising," she answered honestly.

"I'd like to hear more. It obviously pleased you. Perhaps as we walk back to the Miranda?"

Lynn jumped up, and seeing that they were going Dan came across and walked to the door.

"Going already? Boss should be here any time now. His plane was due . . ."

Clive's fingers bit into Lynn's arm so that she lost Dan's words. Next she heard him answering Clive.

"Yes, Bossiney O'Connell, my brother."

They said cheerio. "We'll be seeing you," Clive said and he almost ran Lynn down the alley. "Does this make us one step ahead?" he asked and there was an exultant note in his voice.

12

"LET'S work out what it means," Clive said in a low exultant voice. "We know the identity of the Boss. And we know O'Connell's is part of the set-up. Now, are we one step ahead? I think so."

Lynn listened without being able at the moment to assess what this information meant. She felt stunned. It had come out of the blue and she wasn't used to taking information in that way. It was part of Clive's job, but she was new to it.

She tried to set her brain to work. The Boss was arriving soon. Dan had given them the information that they wanted of Charles Edgar and Joan Tracey. Why? What was his game?

She voiced her doubts but Clive had that worked out. "It's pretty clear that we are looked on as part of the racket . . . or at least wanting to get on the wagon. It explains some of the observation we've felt focussed on us. It could explain Marco."

"Um . . ." Lynn didn't feel too happy

because she felt it was right. If that's what they were taken to be . . . She shivered but didn't let Clive see.

"Probably," he was saying thoughtfully as he examined the likely possibilities, "we could be marked as the successors to Charles Edgar—or I could."

"Oh, no," Lynn protested.

He ignored her. "Let's hope it's that and we're not suspect. They've got to be pretty wary. But I'd say we've covered our traces . . ." His voice died and he went into a silent study. On balance he thought they were not suspect.

Lynn's mind was on Joan Tracey. Now the showdown was on them she was deeply concerned. What would be her reactions when she learned the truth about Charles Edgar? As a person she must be horrified but as a woman? Could she help her feelings? Perhaps he represented all that she had longed for when she broke from the stuffiness of home?

Lynn looked at Clive and asked herself, Would it make any difference to her feelings if he were a criminal? It was no good telling herself she'd known what he was too long. Supposing he became a criminal now . . . over this case? Supposing the money proved too strong a temptation? Would she cease loving him?

Perhaps for the first time Lynn realised that she was really in love with Clive Hendon. She put out her hand and took his as they walked.

Presently Clive talked. He was making plans. "I want to see this Boss fellow before he sees me."

Lynn was immediately attentive.

"I'll go back to O'Connell's after dinner." Lynn was going to protest but he wasn't prepared to listen. "I must keep one step ahead. I want to weigh up the fellow."

"But . . . Dan will tell him who you are." Lynn was holding his hand convulsively but he seemed unaware of her grip.

"I shan't advertise my presence. I shan't go in."

Lynn knew some relief.

"I'll go up and drift around."

"We can go to the plateau and work down . . ."

"You can't. You're not in on this."

Lynn bridled. "It's my case as much as yours."

"Spare me." He glared at her. "You know darn well it isn't. I won't say you haven't been a help. You've helped with the tourist image. I couldn't have projected that without you. But from now on the job is mine."

She began to argue.

He refused to listen. "This isn't a time for petticoat government. You've got your job and it isn't tagging along behind me."

Lynn swallowed and held back the protests. He'd not listen.

"*If* anything should happen that I don't get back to the Miranda by daybreak tomorrow, you are to ignore the rendezvous on the harbour and leave at once. Get me? Don't wait for breakfast. Guan will drive you to the airport and you must take the first plane that will get you away . . . via Paris, Brussels, but get on your way. Do you understand."

It was quite plain, Lynn thought with a sick feeling in the pit of her stomach.

"Have you enough money?"

"Yes."

"Put your passport in your handbag— and don't take any luggage."

"I won't leave you," she burst out.

"You probably won't have to," he replied calmly. "This is only an emergency plan. I must be sure you know what to do. You're not used to improvising. You're not trained to jump like a cat in either direction as the situation demands which is part of the technique of this job." He looked at her but Lynn didn't think he was seeing her as a woman only as a responsibility. "You've got it, haven't you." She nodded. "Good. That makes me feel safer."

Her eyes widened.

"I shan't have to think about you if I have to make sudden changes of plan. I'll know you'll be all right."

She couldn't argue. "I'll . . . do what you say."

"Good." He dismissed that part of his planning. "I'll leave after dinner."

It was a specially well-cooked and well-served meal but Lynn didn't appreciate it. She had little idea what she was eating. Her mind was on the sudden quickening of the case. It was as Clive said. Things drifted, it seemed as if nothing was happening and then all of a sudden you were caught up in action. Lynn daren't shudder or he'd ask if she were cold. She wasn't. She was scared for him. He was walking into a situation that looked evil and sinister.

After dinner they went upstairs and he left her in her bedroom. "Wait there," he said. "The lounge is too public."

She gripped his hand. "You will be careful," she begged.

He looked down at her and nodded, momentarily pleased by her concern but his mind was already projected to the job. "I shan't be long. I only want to see the fellow."

Lynn heard his footsteps running downstairs, heard his voice say something cheery in Spanish to Pedro and then she rushed to the balcony to lean over and watch his tall figure disappear. She put her hand over her mouth in an agony of fear.

She'd no idea how long she stood on the balcony looking at the corner round which he'd disappeared, striding off as if he were going to a jaunt. He'd made light of his precautions and made them sound reasonable, but they drummed fearfully in her mind. If he didn't come back by daybreak . . . She licked her lips—there was no lipstick left on them—and clenched her hands; they were clammy.

"Steady," she said and looked at the hotel outside wall. She could smell roses . . . and felt faint. She'd never smell roses without thinking how beautiful they were in March.

Lynn had no idea how long she stood on the balcony. Part of the time her mind was a blank and she experienced only the ache in her heart. If only they could have had a little more time together and she could have let him see that she loved him. Abruptly she turned into the room. What purpose would that have served? He'd never shown any signs of love for her.

She obeyed his instructions, checking that her passport was in her handbag and she had her money. Then she went through it to see that she had all that she would need for a hurried and inconspicuous departure. She decided what she would wear. Holiday clothes that wouldn't give her away.

Abruptly, she pulled herself up. Her thinking was defeatist. She walked on the balcony and stared in the direction Clive had taken. She wouldn't see his return until he was practically at the Miranda.

Time dragged. She went through the odds and ends in her handbag. She looked at her diary and read some of the information. She saw when it was high tide at London Bridge . . . and quite suddenly she couldn't accept this inactivity any longer. She walked into the bedroom, put on a cardigan, went downstairs and out of the Miranda.

She had no plan but she took the road Clive had taken, towards the alley leading to Dan O'Connell's.

It wasn't a long walk and she ran part of the way, keeping a look out so that Clive shouldn't pass her. She went up the alley keeping in the shadow of one wall and looked straight ahead when anyone passed. But no one more than glanced her way. When she saw the light streaming out from Dan's she stopped. What now?

Where was Clive? He'd said he wasn't going into the bar. Holding her breath she looked round wondering if there was anywhere he might hide. But if he were hidden how would he see the Boss?

Lynn's mind went in circles and got her

nowhere. A couple came from Dan's and she slunk back into the shadows. Dare she walk up on the side nearest and look in as she passed?

She was bracing herself when she saw a figure up the alley. He didn't come from the shadows, he hadn't been hiding. She recognised the walk. No one else had that particular nonchalant swagger. He was coming down the lane, hands in pockets.

"Clive," she breathed and caught his arm.

Her voice startled him. For a moment he looked at her as she seized his arm. Then he spoke icily. "What are you doing here?" He was almost choking as he pulled his arm clear and took her elbow to guide her down the alley.

"I couldn't wait any longer."

"Why? What happened?" He was immediately alert.

She looked up at him blankly. "N-nothing."

He was speechless.

"I'm sorry. I couldn't stay there alone." She stumbled a few paces and caught her breath in a sob. She started to cry, helplessly.

"Cripes!" he breathed but made no attempt to stop walking or to comfort her. He dropped her elbow. "It's nerve-racking having to wait. But surely you can see this business is serious? Surely you don't have to be so childish?"

His attitude was what she needed. He was neither sympathetic nor was he really concerned for her feelings.

They walked on in silence, then he took her hand and began talking as if there had been no words between them. "I got a good look at the Boss. I joined a noisy crowd that was milling round, half inside and half out. You know the type. They take over. I put on this." He unrolled a straw hat similar to Guan's. "I managed to have a good look without being noticed and I saw the fellow sitting in the corner we always choose."

"What's he like?"

"He's not big but he looks tough."

"Does . . . he . . ." the words stuck in Lynn's throat. ". . . look a killer?"

"He could be. He's a flashy dresser and I guess the decorations were real . . . ring, watch, you know. What can be jewelled will be. He's obviously not Dan's brother.

I should say there's mixed blood from somewhere in South America."

"You seem to have learned a lot."

"That's part of the job." He paused as they came to the short street that ran along the back of the harbour and looked at the cafés. They were not busy but most had a client or two. "Do you mind if we don't sit where there's anyone else?" he asked.

"You're in charge," she said with the first flash of humour she'd felt since dinner. "You were a long time mingling with that crowd to see the Boss or did you have to wait for them?"

"No. They were there soon after I was. I walked up to the plateau to the hotel and had a drink."

Lynn felt herself withdraw. To go and have a drink while she was waiting, stewing in a sweat of fear for his safety . . . "I got the receptionist to put through a call to Ellis."

Lynn's temper vanished.

"I got over to him that the big day is tomorrow. He's in the picture. It was a private phone room as you may remember."

Lynn didn't although they had been in

225

the hotel. She hadn't noticed but as Clive said she was an amateur.

"I think I can see the set-up now," Clive was saying.

She held his hand, conscious that they were together, and conscious with an ache somewhere in her middle that he wasn't aware of her except as a listener.

"Dan's place is one of the gang's clearing houses, chiefly for meetings and messages I'd say. He may sometimes have the stuff there. At any rate it's a link in the chain and our work here will eventually smash the whole rotten business." Clive spoke with satisfaction.

"Who are you working for?" Lynn asked suddenly.

"Hendon's," he replied simply, but deliberately.

"You're not being employed by anybody are you?"

"The wife got in touch with us to find Charles Edgar so that she can get a divorce."

"But she's not paying you to uncover the drug people."

"Well, no, that's sort of gratuitous." He spoke off-handedly, and Lynn knew that this part of the work was being undertaken by the brothers because it had to be done by somebody. Nobody was paying them. "It'll be good publicity."

Lynn smiled widely. How she knew that playing-down streak in Clive.

"Tomorrow," he went on, "I'll spot Charles Edgar and Joan Tracey—I'll be down here early to see them arrive."

"We will."

"We will what?"

"Be down here early," she replied and grew taut for the struggle that she saw was ahead. He would keep her out of everything now if he could.

He didn't reply immediately. They'd turned looking for a café into a public garden where the palms were tall and there were seats for lovers by beds of exotic and brightly coloured flowers.

"Ye-es, you'll have to be there because of Joan," he said.

They walked through the gardens to the rocky land beyond which was almost the end of Flavidest's small cove. The wind was increasing and the dark navy sea was flecked with white horses.

Clive slipped his arm round her waist

and Lynn turned to him with a release of tension and an upsurge of emotion that was overwhelming. She was in his arms, her face lifted for his kisses. If he hesitated it was only for another second.

Lynn gave herself fully to the moment. Her love was completely his.

But he released her. "No, Lynn . . . you're making me forget Jack."

"But . . ."

He kissed her lightly, and without passion and lifting her off her feet he turned her round and they started the walk back to the Miranda.

Later Lynn hugged herself in bed, not to keep warm but to enjoy her thoughts. Clive hadn't found it easy to think of Jack!

She woke to the sound of bells proclaiming Sunday.

She had a shower and dressed, putting on the white frock, green sandals and green beads and looking with satisfaction at the whole. She had a sun-tan that brought out the colours of her eyes and her dark hair looked full of lights. She was pleased with the result but she was aware of an uneasiness and a knowledge that she would be glad when today was over and

Finis would be written across the Tracey and Charles Edgar files. For that reason she was down to breakfast early, eager to get on with the job. She'd no idea how it would work out. Had Clive? He had made his plans. Now Ellis knew that the Boss was here and known, he would probably send a man with authority to enlist the local police and apprehend Bossiney O'Connell. Clive believed he was to be offered a job in the racket and on that evidence the Boss could be taken.

What of Joan and Charles Edgar? Lynn couldn't see her way. Clive might be satisfied but to her there seemed a lot of ifs and buts.

He was waiting for her, cheerfully unperturbed in a yellow and green checked shirt. He was certainly playing his part of the typical tourist. Lynn couldn't believe they'd had several days of holiday together. It seemed like a dream now.

"It's windy as I expect you've noticed." It wasn't as fierce as that famous Wednesday, but it was too windy to have breakfast on the terrace. The sea was a wonderful blue, chopped with white and coming up the beach in breakers that the wind caught into spray.

It was windy but it was warm so Lynn carried her cardigan as they set off for the harbour soon after half past nine. Clive hadn't said much about her going but he had emphasised that she was under orders. "We don't know what to expect. We are going to meet Joan and the Edgar fellow and somehow you are going to take Joan with you. That's what it looks like. What will transpire may be out of our reckoning."

He was to prove right.

But he talked on, enlarging on those lines. That was the way he thought the pattern would work out. He would prevent the Boss from getting Charles Edgar on his own. "And somehow I must keep the Boss under surveillance until Ellis's man gets here."

There was a certain vagueness about the set up that increased Lynn's uneasiness as they walked to the harbour. She hated the thought that she would have to leave Clive when she had made contact with Joan Tracey and take her to the Miranda. From there Clive had given her instructions to leave during the afternoon to catch the evening plane "whatever is or is not happening elsewhere. Got it? It's an order." He repeated it as they walked.

There was a Sunday atmosphere round the harbour where some families were "mucking about in boats." There were quite a number of small private yachts. "I shouldn't think they'll be able to put to sea today," Lynn remarked.

Clive looked at the waves and shrugged. "It may not be as bad as it looks."

There was no one along the long harbour arm except a man fishing at the far end.

"We're early," Clive remarked and there was a clipped note in his voice that had been absent all the week but that told her he was keyed up for all his nonchalant appearance. "We'll walk up and see if the fellow has caught anything."

They did so unhurriedly. Every now and again Lynn looked round to see if Joan and Charles Edgar were coming and found herself looking at the cars that were beginning to fill the parking space.

The fisherman showed his catch and then Clive and Lynn strolled back towards the land. It was time the other couple turned up. Lynn felt her heartbeats quickening in spite of her efforts to be calm.

She was staring fixedly at the cars travelling along the road when she was aware that a boatman was addressing Clive from a motor vessel moored to the steps. They weren't the steps she and Clive had disembarked from with Guan but were nearer the sea.

Clive answered him in Spanish and turned to Lynn with a sudden gleam in his eyes.

"He says he's from Dan."

She drew back and looked to see if the Boss were there, but the small cabin cruiser looked empty.

"So . . ." Clive breathed and motioned Lynn to go down the steps and on board. He cut short her protests. "It's as you thought at the beginning. The island."

Reluctantly Lynn allowed herself to be ushered aboard. She supposed Clive must have weighed up what it was all about. She would have liked time to think.

Clive didn't follow for some minutes but stood on the steps talking to the man, then followed Lynn into the small cabin and told her that Joan Tracey and Charles Edgar were on the island. "It's as you thought," he said again, and his eyes looked keen as he began to adjust his thoughts to meet this development.

Lynn watched him and then slipped to the door of the cabin and stood braced to meet the sea. It was a rough journey with the small boat straining against the churning sea and it exhilarated her. There was something stimulating about the pull of the engines and the man's sure hand on the wheel. The spray came up in bursts but the bow protected her. "It's like being in a submarine," she laughed though she'd never been in one.

She enjoyed the rough sea so tried to sink her misgivings at the turn of events. She trusted Clive. He was in charge as he'd said. Nevertheless as the shore fell away and the island began to look closer she was uneasy. It looked as if this move had taken the initiative from Clive.

He came and stood behind her and she leaned back to feel him against her. "It's grand," he said.

He'd made his plans. "We'll bring Joan and Edgar straight back."

"What about the Boss?"

"He's not likely to be there yet."

Lynn jerked up her head. "There's something wrong somewhere." The little ship was facing the island now; it had loomed up like a land mass.

He pulled away from her.

"Of course there is. I don't know what it is, but I can feel it." She looked at the churning sea beating up against the rocks of the island and wondered where there was a landing place. Then it came into sight, the small stone jetty on the right of the sandy cove that looked more like part of the rock formation than man made.

Clive ignored her. He went forward and talked with the boatman who nodded then he came back reassuring. "We've got to find Joan and Edgar. They're not likely to be as much in the know as we are. It's my guess that Edgar knows the Boss will come sometime, and that he and Joan have been waiting here, camping out."

"We didn't see any sign of them."

"They'd hardly have been likely to show themselves unless they were sure it was the

Boss. I'll go ashore and find them. The chap says he will be waiting, for the journey back."

"Why can't we go back in the Boss's boat?" Lynn had to throw her voice against the wind.

The boat came up to the jetty and the man threw a rope and leapt out after it, skilfully seizing it and twisting it round an iron stake that had been driven into the rocks.

As he pulled the boat alongside Clive jumped ashore and began to walk off, looking round and up at the cliffs. Somehow he had got to persuade Charles Edgar that he was a friend.

Pictures flashed through Lynn's mind with startling clarity. Why should Charles Edgar think Clive was a friend? Was he? Wasn't he indirectly a representative of the law? Was it likely Charles Edgar would be unarmed?

With a cry, "I'm coming," she jumped ashore and began scrambling up the rocks after him.

It was when she came to him as he paused to take his bearings that they both looked down and saw the boat leaving the jetty.

For the first time Clive betrayed some emotion. He sought and found her hand and his grip was vice-like. And for the first time Lynn heard him swear.

They were being left, marooned.

13

THE boat that had brought them to the island was only a few yards out to sea as the boatman manoeuvred to get her out of the bay and clear of the jetty as the waves caught her, but she might have been a mile away for all the difference it made to Lynn and Clive. There was no mistaking the object of the action.

They were marooned on the island.

For several moments neither fully realised what that meant. Then Clive began to swear under his breath as he walked a few steps towards the beach.

Lynn followed and shook her head in amazement. Clive had the ciné camera to his eye and was filming the boat's departure even while he was calling himself names. As she came up to him she saw that he was white round the mouth and that his eyes were grey and narrowed.

"Of all the damn fools," he said and Lynn knew he was referring to himself.

Even so he was on the job. "Get out of the way," he snapped as Lynn wandered on a few paces and her head obscured his view.

She jumped out of the way and bit back an angry retort. Instinctively she felt for him. At the same time the seriousness of their predicament began to seep into her brain and she made herself study it without emotion. If they were truly marooned they would eventually starve. At the moment the thought was logical rather than emotional because she didn't feel hungry and she couldn't imagine doing so.

Clive was still taking his pictures though the boat was well clear of the island. Lynn concentrated on him, and waited sympathetically as he lowered the camera and stared towards the mainland. He was the leader of this expedition. What was he feeling, thinking—and planning? Lynn's feelings were kaleidoscopic and she felt pretty useless at the moment.

Suddenly he turned on her and Lynn fell back a few paces. As she did so she found she had become suddenly calm. He was distraught and for the moment not in control of himself. That fact brought her the feeling of quiet.

He walked to the beach and took off his jacket. Lynn ran after him. "What do you think you're going to do?" Her voice was firm and demanded an answer.

He threw his coat at her and the camera. She dropped them on a rock.

"Don't be so ridiculous. You couldn't swim the distance in a calm sea, let alone in this."

"I'll get to a boat."

"I won't be left."

They stared at one another.

"Don't be so ridiculous," she said again and could have bitten back the words. When a man was stricken by failure he didn't need reminding of the fact. She picked up his coat and buried her face in it. Muffled she said. "I'm sorry, but you frightened me. I can't be left, Clive . . ."

He took his coat and put it on. He didn't answer but Lynn relaxed. "It's Sunday," she said.

"Eh?" His mind was working "nineteen to the dozen" and he got there. "Of course. There are bound to be more people about. I wonder . . ." He took her hand, picking up the camera. "Let's get up on those cliffs and reconnoitre. We can see all the coast there. If this wind follows Wednesday's pattern it should have dropped by midday and then possibly this afternoon there'll be some holiday trips. Or there's the fishing fleet tonight. Guan said there were good fishing grounds to the south-west. Come on." He forged up pulling her after him, oblivious of her stumbling.

He was in control of himself again and of the situation, and to her relief Lynn's calm remained. There was no immediate cause for panic. It might only be like the lull before the storm, but it was a breathing space. They reached one of the highest points and stared south out to sea and then round the great bay. Here the sea was rough and there were no small boats in sight. "But this afternoon, when it's calmer, there'll be more shipping." Clive spoke confidently. "I don't think we'll stand here. It's a cool wind."

Lynn agreed and was glad to move to the shelter of some rocks and feel the sun warm on her.

Clive spoke quietly. "I'm sorry, Lynn. It's a bad show on my part."

"Of course it isn't." She spoke warmly. "It's just one of those things and we weren't one jump ahead as we hoped."

He smiled ruefully. "We certainly were not. I could kick myself. I walked us both into this trap with eyes wide open."

"Have you any idea what the idea is?" she asked diffidently.

"No, it puzzles me. At the moment I can't see any pattern. It can't be blackmail, or he'd have bargained with us—to take us ashore for some exorbitant sum."

Clive had a grip on himself again, and although Lynn was aware of the graveness of their predicament she felt content to sit in the sun staring at the mainland.

"It must have been Dan's idea. What did the boatman say when he came up to us?"

"He spoke in Spanish."

"That's right. I wonder if I misunderstood? He said the friend I wanted would be on the island. I thought he meant Charles Edgar and Joan. We've had the idea they might be using the island as a hide-out. Did I jump to conclusions on a preconceived idea?"

Lynn didn't answer. He didn't want one.

"Where does the Boss come in this?"

In spite of her calm Lynn shivered.

"At the moment there's not a glimmer of light." Clive sat forward, elbows on knees, chin cupped in his hands.

"What about Charles Edgar and Joan?" Lynn asked at last. "They're supposed to be on the island."

"Ye-es," Clive agreed but he didn't move. He sat chewing his top lip. Then; slowly he looked round at the rocks rising above them. There were caves where a man could hide, he'd remarked. "Let's walk down to the beach and look up, carefully and see if we can see anything." He laughed sharply. "We're rather like sitting ducks here."

Lynn's eyes widened.

"Charles Edgar may be armed, and he may not see us as colleagues."

He pulled her to the left and helped her down the rough way to the small bay. They walked to the water's edge and then looked back up the sloping face of the

cliffs with their crevices and slits, pre-
cariously growing bushes and outcrops of
tufty grass and weeds. Slowly Clive's eyes
travelled from one side to the other and
then back again at a different level.

Lynn's did the same. "He's probably
well hidden."

"But it should be possible to see some
tell-tale marks." But at last he had to
shake his head. "If they're here they've
not done much coming and going on this
side of the island."

"Perhaps they were afraid of being
picked up by the telescopes at Flavidest."

"Possibly," he agreed brightening.
"Let's just have a look here." He went to
the tumbledown shed. It had once been a
serving kiosk, Clive decided, with a small
kitchen at the back. "It was never much
more. I shouldn't say any one has ever
lived in it even for the summer."

"Guan said there was no water."

"That's right." I should think ice creams
and imported minerals are brought over on
the days the boatmen visit the island. No
one has been poking round here recently."
He straightened his back suddenly. "Keep
your eyes on the right of the rocks while I

cover the left. I'm going to shout and see if I can startle the fellow into making some movement and betraying himself." He bent down as if examining some debris and then straightening swiftly let out a ringing shout. "Hey . . . Charles Edgar!"

Lynn stared, her eyes covering the side assigned her and her heartbeats quickening. Several birds rose, but there was nothing else.

Clive drew a blank, too, and a silence settled on the island that seemed separate from the pounding of the sea.

What now? Lynn wondered.

"Let's find a sheltered spot," Clive said and indicated a rock that would be comfortable and sunny and out of the wind, but Lynn realised the shelter that Clive meant was from observation from anyone hiding above them. Overhanging cliff and clinging trees sheltered them from above.

Clive began to re-cap, vaguely.

"You don't have to water down the position for me," Lynn stopped him.

"No . . . I ought to have realised you can take it."

Her heart seemed to jump with a

wonderful joy. This was the first time Clive had ever praised her character. "Go on," she said and sat with her elbows tight into her sides, and determined to get every ounce out of what he was saying to make relevant remarks and helpful suggestions. "What is likely to happen?"

"I really don't know, Lynn. That's the devil of it. I've miscalculated. We've been lured here. Why? Because Dan O'Connell thinks we want to get in on the drug racket. That would seem to be fair reasoning. But it's phoney somewhere. I'm dead sure of that but I can't see where. Why should they want to get us here with Charles Edgar and ladyfriend? I'm sure my information that the Boss is going to kill Charles Edgar is reliable. Why have us as witnesses?"

Lynn shivered.

"I know." He put his arm round her. "It's horrifying."

"What about Joan?" Lynn asked. "What will the Boss do to her?"

Clive's lips were dry. He licked them and shook his head. "Who knows what's in his mind?" And Lynn knew he was thinking about her and himself. What were the Boss's plans for them? Witnesses of murder . . .

"I suppose he'll come from Flavidest," Clive remarked and Lynn had no need to ask who. She realised from their position as well as being sheltered from being a target for Charles Edgar they could see anyone approaching the jetty.

For a time, they sat in silence. Lynn was still trying to see if there was any significant fact Clive had overlooked or that she had failed to extract from her conversations with Ellis.

Suddenly he turned on her. "It's your fault," he said bluntly.

Lynn was too taken aback to protest, she looked at him dazedly. He meant what he was saying, but as she recovered he went on, with a half grin.

"If I hadn't been head over heels in love with you I'd have kept my mind on what I was doing instead of thinking about you nearly all the time."

Lynn gaped and the blood rushed to her head, or somewhere, and she felt as if she were being enwrapped in a wave of happiness.

"It's a fact. I'd have been behaving properly, seeing clearly . . ."

"I think you behaved very properly," she murmured.

He glared. "Don't take the mickie. It's a fact. Your being around warped my judgement."

Lynn looked at him in wondering amazement and for the moment couldn't think of anything but the meaning of the words that rang in her ears, "If I hadn't been head over heels in love with you!" Clive—he was head over heels in love with her. "Oh darling," she whispered.

"For heaven's sake," he protested, "don't make it any harder."

"I'm not. I can't help being natural, can I?" she flashed.

"It's not like that, Lynn, a holiday proximity promoting an affair of moonlight and music . . ."

"And March roses," she murmured.

"What have they got to do with it?" he asked after a moment's stunned silence while he looked at her expression with increasing disbelief.

"Nothing and yet everything. They seem part of the magic."

247

"Huh, magic," he nodded. "That's what I was saying it's *not*. It's plain fact." He looked at her, from the tip of her green sandals to the top of her dark hair. "I couldn't—I can't get you out of my mind."

She put her hand on his where it rested palm downwards on the rock. "And your heart?" she prompted.

"What about it?"

"Is it involved?"

"Oh, for gracious sake . . ." He looked at her sighing and then their eyes held and his lit with incredulous hope. "Lynn, you don't really mean . . . ? Cripes."

"Me, too," she admitted, "only I'd have said it was my heart that was over-burdened with you."

"Heart and mind it's all of me," he grunted, "and it's some burden!" But she'd had enough of words and taking her hand off his was holding out her arms. He caught her to him and held her, and his eyes were almost all blue she noticed before he began kissing her.

The wind was gentle in this sheltered spot and the sea swept in with a sound like music, but the moment that was theirs was short. "We must think, darling," he broke away.

"How can we?" she protested but agreed. She knew it could be a matter of life and death. Clive loved her. She shook her head and thought how blind she'd been all those years in the office. She was about to tease him with being blind, too, when she felt something in the back of her mind, as if she were going to think of something and she listened in silence as he talked aloud, trying to see his way through their predicament.

"All the facts as we know them don't make sense. The Boss. Dan O'Connell and his place as a clearing station, a link in the ring. Charles Edgar and Joan Tracey . . ."

Lynn went suddenly dead cold. In a flash she had the idea that had been disturbing her. "Clive, what if Dan has mistaken us for Charles Edgar and Joan?"

"Good heavens, no."

"He could," she insisted, a cold feeling round her heart.

"But he's a little chap, or at least of medium height," he looked at his long legs, "and she's fair. We know that from the photos and Mrs. Tracey's description."

"Does Dan know that? Supposing Charles Edgar and Joan have never stayed here? Couldn't he have imagined we were the couple trying to contact the Boss. Couldn't . . ."

"Be quiet a minute."

Without rancour she sat quietly while he examined the idea. "Like heck I hope you're wrong," he said at last and stood up. "You realise this is the Boss's chosen killing ground."

Feeling sick she nodded.

"Sorry to be blunt, Lynn, but we've got to face facts. We've got to see clearly now or we may never have the chance to see clearly in future. Oh, darling, if only I'd waited to fall in love."

Her longing was to tell him what a wonderful thing it was he had at anytime but she held back the words and, smiling, got to her feet and took his hand, waiting for his decision.

"I don't mind telling you, I'm uncertain. I think . . . I think we'd better get to the other side of the island and see if

250

there's any hope of getting off that way, or any place in which we really can hide."

They skirted the island round the low ground jumping from rock to rock avoiding pools and stared out across the sea.

"It looks awfully empty."

"But the sea isn't as rough," he said and looked fixedly to the left. "I believe . . . yes, it is a motor lauuch. There, can you see?"

Lynn followed the direction and saw the spray sweeping up in a double plume. "They're coming this way!"

"Yes." His voice was hoarse as he started to scramble up the rocks and began to wave. "It's no good shouting they'll never hear anything in this wind, but they may see us." Nevertheless he shouted and so did Lynn.

The boat came closer. Were they on a trip round the island? Lynn clenched her hands and scrambled up beside Clive, and stood there waving and yelling. Her sandals were soaked and the skirt of her frock was wet. Clive's slacks were clinging round his legs.

The boat drove nearer. "They're coming this way," Clive yelled.

They were holding hands but Lynn had no idea how tight she was grasping him until she glanced down and saw the whites of her knuckles.

"They've seen us!"

It was true. Two of the passengers had seen them and were waving. One of them told the man at the wheel and he looked towards them and waved and turned the boat, but he didn't come very near. He passed the island and turned to go round it.

"They can't pick us up here," Clive shouted. "There's only that landing spot on the other side." He gave Lynn his hand and stumbling and falling they raced round to the other side. The boat had swung out in an arc and was coming towards them. The two passengers standing up were waving, the boatman gave them a salute and then with a spectacular swing that sent up the waves behind him he headed back to Flavidest.

Lynn buried her head in the front of Clive's jacket.

"They probably thought we're out for

the day and are here by choice," he said flatly. "But there are bound to be others."

Lynn made no attempt to stop her tears. They were the result of the pent up emotion of the last hour as well as this disappointment. She clung to him and his arms were round her. "There are bound to be others," he said.

She made murmuring noises of acquiescence.

She wasn't looking but she could see in imagination the desolation of the island. The bare rocks and the sparse patches of green, the all-powerful sea cutting it off from man, the grandeur of it and the frightening isolation.

She was deeply aware of love and of fear. She had never felt so frightened in her life and she knew it wasn't a foolish fear, a matter of bogies in the dark. She knew she couldn't wake up and find it had all been a nightmare.

As she held to Clive she felt his lean body and the tautness of it. Bitterly she thought that it was his falling in love with her, the loveliest thing that could have happened that had made him vulnerable and caused him to fail in his job. She didn't question that he had, he would have been more aware of what was happening and likely to occur if he hadn't been so aware of her. She thought how they had drifted and of the warm pleasure of those few holiday-fied days.

With an effort she pulled away and stood upright. He was stern-faced and pale and there was sweat along his forehead.

As taut as he was she felt him stiffen even more. "There's a boat coming," he said hoarsely.

"Here?" She stared at it. Of course it was coming to the island and she knew her question was silly immediately she'd asked it. "If it's the Boss he's come to kill."

Clive didn't contradict. "I wonder . . . He knows Charles Edgar. He'll know I'm not his man. I wonder if I can bluff him that we are trippers, simply that, and that Dan has gaffed? He knows there are two of us here . . ." He looked down at her asking himself if she ought to hide or stay by him.

"Let's both hide!" The words burst from Lynn.

"Ye-es. It might be an idea. It'll give us time. And time can be valuable." They turned from the beach and climbed up by the jetty towards the caves. At a difficult spot Lynn reached out for the hand Clive was holding to her, and screamed.

A man behind Clive was facing them with a gun.

14

AS Lynn screamed Clive dropped her hand and whipped round. She felt as if the world were tottering and for a moment she threatened, though she didn't know it, to faint. This was too much. But the feeling passed and left her shaking, facing this development with trembling limbs and a fearful heart.

Clive was staring at the man. She couldn't see his expression but knew it must be dumbfounded at first and then imagined the consternation. He cleared his throat but no words came.

Lynn stood stiffly and as so often happens when one is frightened time seemed to stand still, and the moments when they stood rigid were for ever etched on Lynn's memory.

"My name is Charles Edgar." The man, of medium build looked tough and alert, and his narrowed dark brown eyes missed nothing. "I see you know the name."

He spoke with a North country accent

and held the revolver without a tremor. He wouldn't hesitate to use it.

"Yes." Clive's voice was quiet. Lynn stepped up beside him and took his hand, keeping her eyes on Charles Edgar. He didn't look flabby like a man who had been in prison. He looked bronzed, lean and powerful. He could have been menacing even without the gun.

"Where's Joan?" she asked impulsively.

"I don't take women on man-hunting trips."

Clive caught his breath and Lynn saw the colour stain and flush his fair cheeks. She squeezed his hand and ignored the crack. "Is she all right? I'll have to report to her mother."

She saw a gleam in the man's eyes but couldn't read its meaning, nevertheless she found herself breathing more easily.

Charles Edgar did not measure up to her picture of him. She had seen him in her imagination as something less than human. This was a man. He fitted the picture physically, even to the scar on his nose and forehead. Lynn was puzzled. Charles Edgar was a thoroughly bad egg; she felt he had no right to have this clean, wholesome look. Uneasily she moved closer to Clive, aware she was being influenced by appearances.

She looked round, only turning her head slightly to watch the sea splashing in over the rocks. It had lost some of its power, and the wind had slackened.

The sea becoming calmer, was in tune with her feelings, she thought in surprise. Part of her accepted the fact that she and Clive were faced with an ugly situation. This man was Clive's enemy and he had the upperhand. But she felt calm inside. She supposed that once the worst had happened one began to accept it. Was it escapism?

She found hope in the fact that Charles Edgar was a human-seeming human being . . .

He barked out an order. "You've got a camera. Use it as the Boss comes in to land."

Obediently Clive put the camera to his eye, looked through it and lowered it. Lynn looked hard in the direction of Flavidest, for the Boss's boat. Charles Edgar was watching them both. He was hidden from anyone landing at the jetty, so his span of vision was limited.

"Is that his boat?" Lynn asked. The small launch was carving its way towards the island.

Charles Edgar didn't answer. He made no attempt to expose himself.

"It could be," Clive replied and when she opened her mouth to speak again, she felt she must chatter—he frowned her to silence. For a moment her feelings went ragged but she suddenly saw that he must be concentrating on their predicament. Her nattering was an irritant. Quietly she stood beside him watching the launch come nearer.

"Well?" Charles Edgar asked.

"A launch is heading this way. As far as I can see there is only one man on board," Clive answered.

"He wouldn't want any witnesses."

Lynn jumped. So Charles Edgar knew the Boss was a killer?

"Step out and go on using your ciné, not particularly on him though I want the best pictures you can get, but touristwise. Let him see you . . ."

"No," Lynn protested.

"Be quiet," Clive ordered. "I've got the hang. I'll step out—on one condition."

"Well?"

"That you swear no hurt shall come to Lynn."

The man laughed. "That's a tall order. Women are too unpredictable."

"She's only here because she wants to help your girl-friend . . ."

"My wife."

Clive swallowed and nodded. "Well?" he asked in his turn.

"Okay. She'll be all right."

"I don't want to be," Lynn snapped not really knowing what she was saying. "Nothing is to happen to Clive. Nothing." Her voice rose hysterically as if by the depth of her passion she would force Charles Edgar to give his protection to Clive.

"Cut it," Clive growled and walked away from the rocks and slowly down towards the beach.

"Go with him," Charles Edgar ordered, "and keep out of sight till he's ashore. Then go to meet him—both of you."

The launch was skilfully manoeuvred into the bay and brought alongside the jetty. The Boss was alone and was as Clive had described him. He was flashily dressed even in these circumstances and very sure of himself. He was an expert seaman and came alongside, tied up and stood on the quay with a revolver, all in a few minutes.

Clive was holding Lynn's hand. He gave it a firm squeeze, murmuring, "Now for it, play naturally," and walked into sight. He laughed and they looked like any happy holiday couple.

"Who the hell are you?" the Boss barked, and asked the question again in a language Lynn didn't understand. "Where's Charles Edgar?"

Clive walked forward and lifted his hand as if in greeting. He knows what he's doing Lynn thought exultantly and walked almost buoyantly beside him.

The Boss held his revolver ready. "Well? You're not Charles Edgar and his moll. He's a short chap . . ." He swore, cursed Dan for his mistake realising that he'd been betrayed.

Lynn felt a wave of sickness as a shot rang out and instinctively she dropped her head in her hands.

Clive stood stiffly by her side.

Lynn gaped. The Boss had dropped his gun and was holding his arm looking at the blood on his hand, stupified.

Charles Edgar had fired.

"Thanks, mister," Clive grinned as Edgar joined them. "I don't know who you are, but I do know you're not Charles Edgar."

That's what she knew, Lynn thought and had known subconsciously ever since she had seen him as so human.

The Boss was scrambling back to his boat. Charles Edgar had no time to answer; he made a sharp rush forward, followed by Clive, and brought the Boss down.

With a minimum of fuss and practically no words the Boss was tied up and bundled on to the launch. Actually, Lynn thought she and Clive were in no better position than they had been. They were still at the mercy of a man with a gun, but she felt happy. It might be ridiculous, but she was content. As she had thought earlier, she liked the look of Charles Edgar whoever he was.

"Are you going to take us back with

you?" she asked as she walked along the jetty and jumped into the launch.

"I don't seem to have any choice," he answered straightfaced.

Lynn glanced at the Boss, trussed and gagged at the stern of the boat and stood a little to the side by the wheel waiting for Clive to join her.

"Wind's dropped," Charles Edgar remarked as he started the launch and, edged her away from the jetty.

He's not too sure of what he's doing, Lynn guessed, but he got the launch away and headed for the open sea.

Reaction threatened and she found herself trembling. So that she shouldn't make a fool of herself she walked to the side and sat on the seat running along it. Then stared at her sandals, dark green with the wet. She didn't feel like using her brain to work out what had happened. She only wanted to rejoice at their miraculous delivery. Clive was standing beside their rescuer, staring straight ahead. What was he thinking?

He had come from London to bring this man face to face with his past . . . Not this man. Who on earth was he? And what about Joan Tracey? He knew her and had called her his wife. "Who are you?" she asked him.

He smiled and took a deep breath before replying as if he wasn't sure what to tell or how to begin. Clive turned to listen. "My friends usually call me John."

"All right—John," Lynn urged him on.

He looked at Clive. "We've been on the same case. I'm afraid I've been your red-herring."

Clive's mouth dropped and Lynn's heart went to him. He was going to be made to feel a fool in a minute. He *had* mucked up the case. She stood up and went to his side. If it hadn't been for her and their love he would have seen clearly. He wouldn't have boobed.

"Go on," Clive's voice sounded dry.

"It amazed us how you got on to the case and were willing to continue it without any financial backing," John said admiringly.

Clive shrugged but Lynn felt his pleasure.

John told the tale and it made sense, the odd pieces of the puzzle fell into place. Charles Edgar had not been released early from prison. That had been a deliberate rumour circulated in the right places.

"Where is he now?" Clive asked.

"Living quietly in London. He was released at the right time. I should think he'll try and go straight. He must know he's not much chance in the drug game. I took his place so that we could get our hands on this . . ." he nodded towards the Boss. "Charles Edgar was small fry."

He concentrated on the launch. The island had fallen behind, Flavidest was coming near.

"Good work," Clive said laconically and Lynn's heart swelled with love. There were still a lot of details to be explained but the main outline was clear. The authorities had been determined to break the drug ring and they had succeeded with John impersonating Charles Edgar and leading the Boss to reveal himself. "You must have been one step ahead all the time."

"Yes. Now, how do I check our speed?" He looked down and Lynn felt the launch respond and slacken. Not skilfully, but adequately, John brought them alongside the harbour. "Wait a jiff, I'll jump out and pull her to the steps."

He did so and Lynn stepped ashore, helped by Clive.

A tall fair girl came to meet them. Joan Tracey, Lynn guessed and smiled when they were introduced. She would be able to tell Mrs. Tracey that Joan was very well indeed.

Clive helped John with their prisoner—pre-arrangements had been made with the local police—while Lynn sat on the harbour wall with Joan.

"There's a lot I still don't understand," Lynn confessed.

"We-ell . . . I don't really know what you know."

Lynn told her what she had uncovered when she'd taken over the case.

Joan's face clouded as she heard about her parents' concern. "I was in a cleft stick. I had to choose, so I chose John," she said simply.

Lynn nodded and thought about herself. She would have to stand firm whatever her mother's reactions to Clive. "The whole thing's a bit of a fog. I gathered you left

London after you'd been friendly with a man in hospital in London . . ."

"That's when they were making the scar on John's nose and forehead," Joan said as if that explained everything.

Lynn looked blank.

Joan smiled and began at the beginning. She had met John when she was working at the hospital and they had fallen in love. "But he was on this secret job. So . . ." Joan lifted her hands in a gesture that said there was no other course open to her. John had gone into hospital to receive the scar to add to his likeness to Charles Edgar. His bodily resemblance was good enough. The rumour was put out that he was a prisoner who'd been beaten up.

"I followed him to the North and then had to disappear. I couldn't be in the picture but we didn't cover our tracks too well."

"No-o. I found out you were here with Charles Edgar."

"When we realised that was known we let it spread so that the Boss's agents were looking for a couple."

"Red herrings," Lynn said of herself and Clive.

"Yes," Joan chuckled. "While we were having a lovely honeymoon along the coast."

Lynn pulled a face at her.

"We were married a few days before John was officially let out of prison. I couldn't go home till we could tell everything so insisted on coming here with John." She watched Lynn kick a pebble off the harbour into the sea. "I think that's about all."

Lynn thought it was. She saw how the unknown bits fitted. She was right that Dan had taken her and Clive for Charles Edgar and Joan who were waiting for the Boss.

"What are you going to do now?" Lynn asked.

"I'm not sure what John has in mind."

"You'll phone your mother." Lynn's words were a statement.

Joan hesitated.

Lynn laughed. "Shall I get through and break the news? If I do may I say you'll phone this evening, and will you promise to do so?"

Joan agreed. "There's no need for secrecy any longer. They'll like John."

Lynn phoned Mrs. Tracey from the Miranda at lunch time. They'd walked along more or less in silence but it wasn't a strain, they were in harmony. Clive had already phoned Ellis and his man would be stopped en route.

When Lynn heard Mrs. Tracey's voice and caught its anxious note she spoke quickly and reassuringly. "I've been talking to Joan this morning, Mrs. Tracey."

"She's all right?"

The line was clear and Lynn didn't think it was imagination that she could hear Mr. Tracey breathing down his wife's neck. Gently she told them that Joan was very happy and that she was looking forward to coming home.

Mrs. Tracey asked quick, gabbled questions.

"Joan's going to phone you herself this evening. I'm phoning now to make sure you will be in and I wanted to let you know directly I'd seen her. Mrs. Tracey . . ." Lynn licked her lips ". . . everything is very good. Joan had to do what she did, about disappearing, I mean. It wasn't her fault really, and she was distressed about having to worry you . . ."

Her voice faded and she heard Mr. Tracey's gruff thanks. Mrs. Tracey was a bit overcome, he said, and cleared his throat noisily. They'd both be in this evening.

"Good work," Clive said as Lynn left the phone. "You've helped them all."

They had their lunch on the terrace. The wind had dropped and it was gloriously calm and sunny.

That evening they went out with John and Joan and sat in a harbour café talking. Joan had phoned her mother. "John was wonderful with her," she said and Lynn smiled as her thoughts went wandering. John wasn't any more wonderful than Clive. Clive had phoned Ellis again and Ellis had said he would phone Mother to say that Lynn would be home tomorrow. It was cold and frosty in London.

She laughed and looked at the creamy pink roses on the wall behind.

Next afternoon she was looking at the mauve crocuses defying the frost and north east wind. They were in the garden round Hamilton Court and Clive was with her.

"Do you want to come into the office tomorrow to write finis on the Tracey file?" he asked.

"I have my own," she replied. Her heart was beating. They were home. What were Clive's plans? He'd never mentioned marriage.

"Your first and . . ." His eyes sought hers.

She waited while she heard the roar of traffic on the road, the screech of brakes as a van failed to beat the lights and some children's voices raised in excited chatter as they came into the garden. It was her last case. She had learned that she had had amateur's luck this time and was grateful. Mrs. Tracey was happy.

"I'll carry your bag up to number five," he said.

Mother opened the door and Lynn was swept into her embrace and the warmth of the flat. Clive went swiftly. It was a disappointing parting but Lynn held his last words to her heart.

"I'll be seeing you."

"Now tell me all about it? Did you enjoy yourself? Did you get any swimming? Was it wonderful in the sun?" Mother asked.

Lynn followed her into the lounge shaking her head and realising that nothing had altered in her absence. The week that had been so momentous to her had been routine at Hamilton Court. She realised, too, that mother saw her visit to Flavidest as more holiday than work.

She laughed and said, surprisingly herself, "We never asked Clive to come in."

Mother's mouth dropped. "Clive? Clive Hendon? Where does he come into the picture?" Mother hadn't recognised him. She'd thought some passing stranger had helped Lynn with her case!

"Everywhere."

Mother listened in silence while they had a cup of tea and Lynn told her tale— most of it. Then she shook her head. Later she told Lynn she was like her father in many ways. "I never could understand him."

Jack rang during the evening. He was in London and ready to date her. "Are you free tomorrow?" he asked in his direct fashion.

"Yes." Clive hadn't asked for a date.

"Good." Jack made a time and a place. "There's a lot to talk about," he said.

Lynn raised her eyebrows and wondered if she were looking forward to seeing Jack. She still liked him . . .

He was pleased to see her. He looked his warm brown self and she felt his warm regard for her. He looked into her eyes and led her to the restaurant where he'd booked a table. He asked about her journey home and the finish of the job in Flavidest.

She told him sketchily and asked about his return from Paris and his parents' trip. Where were they now?

They were going to Italy. "It's us I wanted to talk about."

Lynn tensed.

He chewed the edge of his thumb nail. "I think you're a grand girl, Lynn."

She smiled and tried not to look too encouraging. In an effort to stay him she asked. "Have you heard any more about that plant in Norway?"

He looked amazed. "You must be psychic. That's partly what I wanted to tell you." He stared at the table then looked up and looked directly into her eyes. "I've been offered a job after my own heart back home in connection with the installation of such a plant."

"How marvellous."

"It's the usual five year plan we're working on of course."

Again Lynn tensed.

"I hadn't been reckoning on anything like that . . ."

"But you're thrilled," Lynn guessed and saw the light in his eyes as he nodded.

"I had been hoping," he said, "to settle down but this has made me feel differently. I wouldn't want to get married for five years. It's the sort of job that will take all I've got and mean roughing it. Five years is a long time . . ."

Lynn nodded. "A bit too long," she said gently.

"So this is our farewell, Lynn. I'm going back right away."

She smiled with a happy sense of release. "You can't get off fast enough," she teased and being Jack he took her seriously.

"I wouldn't say that. But if I stayed even a week it would be harder to leave you."

"As we've only got this evening," Lynn re-routed his thoughts, "tell me, untechnically, what this job really means."

He did. The job was a challenge he couldn't resist.

They had a taxi home and as they left it Lynn looked at the flats and made a sudden decision. "Don't come up, Jack. Let's say goodbye here."

They did so. He kissed her and thanked her and wished a little nostalgically that things had been different. "You can't help the way you're made," she told him. "You must follow the way for you," as she was going to follow the way for her.

She watched him back into the taxi and stood until it was out of sight. When it had gone she still stood and presently a tall figure was standing beside her.

"Hallo," she said without turning. She had seen Clive over by a cedar tree as she got out of the taxi.

He put his arm round her waist. "I phoned and your mother told me you were out so I came round and waited."

She guessed that was what had happened. "Aren't you cold?"

"I suppose I am," he said as if he'd not

275

thought of it. "Er-m- Did you have a nice evening with Jack?"

She smiled to herself. "Yes."

"What about me?" he blurted out.

"What about you?" she countered laughing and turning to face him, lifted her face provocatively.

"You can't marry him. I mean. Are you going to marry him—or me?"

"You," she said softly and refused to stand waiting any longer but put her arms up round his neck.

He almost choked and then held her to him as if he'd never let her go.

It was quite a time later when she did release herself.

"It's March. We could be married in April," he said.

"We could. We'd better go and tell mother," she said and took his hand as they walked into the flat and up to number five.

Lynn opened the door and called as she always did when she came home. Her mother opened the lounge door and raised her eyebrows on seeing Clive.

"He's come in for some coffee," Lynn said later as her mother seemed lacking in the laws of hospitality for once, and never even asked him to sit down.

"But . . ."

Lynn laughed. She had gone out with Jack and come home with Clive. "Take off your coat, Clive," she said and smiled fondly at her mother. "I've some wonderful news for you." She sat on the arm of her mother's chair and put her arm round her shoulders. At last she was free of her mother's apron strings. She wasn't sure just when it had happened but she knew for a certainty it had. "Clive and I want to be married next month."

"Oh no . . ." Mother gasped incredulously.

"Oh yes," Lynn replied firmly. "There isn't time this month. You'll want a new hat."

Mary Laurel looked at her daughter and Lynn returned her gaze, then slowly Mary nodded and accepted a new relationship between them.

"I'll make some coffee. But first . . ." She looked at Clive, and smiled. "Do you like it strong? Black or white? I ought to know for future occasions."

He opened the door for her and then

took Lynn in his arms. She knew a deep content. Mother understood. So she relaxed and thought that though there was a lot calling for attention tomorrow would do.

"It won't," Clive contradicted. "We'll fix the date tonight and go house hunting tomorrow . . . when tomorrow is today, if you get me."

Lynn thought she did, and smothered a chuckle. They'd both got each other and she rejoiced in how wonderfully giddy it made you feel to be in love . . . and how intoxicating were kisses.

"The coffee," mother disturbed them and talked about her dress for the wedding. "Blue I think . . ."

Clive's eyes were blue tonight. Lynn smiled into them and her own were starry.

We hope this Large Print edition gives you the pleasure and enjoyment we ourselves experienced in its publication.

There are now more than 2,000 titles available in this ULVERSCROFT Large print Series. Ask to see a Selection at your nearest library.

The Publisher will be delighted to send you, free of charge, upon request a complete and up-to-date list of all titles available.

Ulverscroft Large Print Books Ltd.
The Green, Bradgate Road
Anstey
Leicestershire
LE7 7FU
England

GUIDE
TO THE COLOUR CODING
OF
ULVERSCROFT BOOKS

Many of our readers have written to us expressing their appreciation for the way in which our colour coding has assisted them in selecting the Ulverscroft books of their choice. To remind everyone of our colour coding— this is as follows:

BLACK COVERS
Mysteries

★

BLUE COVERS
Romances

★

RED COVERS
Adventure Suspense and General Fiction

★

ORANGE COVERS
Westerns

★

GREEN COVERS
Non-Fiction

ROMANCE TITLES
in the
Ulverscroft Large Print Series

The Smile of the Stranger	*Joan Aiken*
Busman's Holiday	*Lucilla Andrews*
Flowers From the Doctor	*Lucilla Andrews*
Nurse Errant	*Lucilla Andrews*
Silent Song	*Lucilla Andrews*
Merlin's Keep	*Madeleine Brent*
Tregaron's Daughter	*Madeleine Brent*
The Bend in the River	*Iris Bromige*
A Haunted Landscape	*Iris Bromige*
Laurian Vale	*Iris Bromige*
A Magic Place	*Iris Bromige*
The Quiet Hills	*Iris Bromige*
Rosevean	*Iris Bromige*
The Young Romantic	*Iris Bromige*
Lament for a Lost Lover	*Philippa Carr*
The Lion Triumphant	*Philippa Carr*
The Miracle at St. Bruno's	*Philippa Carr*
The Witch From the Sea	*Philippa Carr*
Isle of Pomegranates	*Iris Danbury*
For I Have Lived Today	*Alice Dwyer-Joyce*
The Gingerbread House	*Alice Dwyer-Joyce*
The Strolling Players	*Alice Dwyer-Joyce*
Afternoon for Lizards	*Dorothy Eden*
The Marriage Chest	*Dorothy Eden*